IMAGINES

IMAGO, BOOK TWO

N.R. WALKER

BLURB

Jack Brighton and Lawson Gale have been together for six months and are very much in love. Lawson's work ensuring the survival of the Tillman Copper is as demanding as ever, and Jack's work with the regeneration of the bushfire-ravaged national park is just as hectic.

When Jack suggests they take a short trip, Lawson agrees. But then he is offered a two-week research position in tropical Queensland to help determine why the Ulysses butterfly is on the decline. Figuring they could combine work and pleasure, Jack and Lawson go on their first vacation together.

Working alongside renowned professor Piers Bonfils isn't easy. But personal and professional differences aside, Lawson is offered a more permanent role in Queensland. Torn between his new life in Tasmania with Jack and a dying species of butterfly he feels compelled to save, Lawson has to decide where his fate lies.

But fate changes the rules. On a research expedition into the depths of the rainforest, suddenly it's not only the butterflies' existence that hangs in the balance.

A butterfly's life cycle never changes. From larvae to imago, their course is plotted by design. Jack and Lawson need to determine where they stand, if they live through it. Because the only thing more incredible than one imago is two.

COPYRIGHT

Cover Artist: Harper By Design
Editor: Labyrinth Bound Edits
Imagines © 2017 N.R. Walker
Publisher: BlueHeart Press

First Edition April 2017

All Rights Reserved:

This literary work may not be reproduced or transmitted in any form or by any means, including electronic or photographic reproduction, in whole or in part, without express written permission except in the case of brief quotations embodied in critical articles and reviews.
This is a work of fiction, and any resemblance to persons, living or dead, or business establishments, events, or locales is coincidental. The Licensed Art Material is being used for illustrative purposes only.

Warning:

Intended for an 18+ audience only. This book contains material that may be offensive to some and is intended for a mature, adult audience. It contains graphic language, explicit sexual content, and adult situations.

The author uses Australian English spelling and grammar.

Trademarks:

All trademarks are the property of their respective owners.

Glossary For Australian Terms

Esky: a portable cooler

Kitchen bench: kitchen counter.

2iC: A person who is 2nd in command/charge.

Ute: (short for utility) Trayback utility

Rouse: (rhymes with house) To scold

DEDICATION

To the folks who watch butterflies, and wonder...

imagines

N.R. WALKER

CHAPTER ONE

THE LANDSCAPE LOOKED BLACKENED and dead, charred beyond any possibility of resurrection. After six months, I would have thought I'd be used to it, but no. It still gave me a moment's pause.

I almost died here. Rosemary too.

Jack almost died here when he'd come to save me.

And that caused my heart to squeeze.

Against all odds, though, like Jack promised it would, there were small signs of new life, new green shoots in the scorched earth. While some trees had sprouted new life, some were nothing but vertical pillars of charcoal, waiting for wind or time to crumble them to nothing.

This land had been cauterised.

All *Bursaria* shrubs were gone; the Tillman Copper butterfly's only known natural habitat in this area had been singed off the face of the planet.

We still had our captive specimens, and they were breeding well. But it wasn't the same. It would never be the same.

Jack came up from the edge of the gully. I could tell by his face but asked anyway. "Any luck?"

He shook his head. "Nah. There's been no activity here since the fire."

I sighed heavily, taking in the cloying scent of burnt earth. Still, after six months, it was all I could smell.

"You hate coming back here, don't you?" Jack asked, putting his hand on my back.

I nodded. "It's not my favourite place."

"You know, for tens of thousands of years, the Aboriginal people used bushfires as a way to encourage new growth." Jack's gaze never left mine. "It's a cycle, and it means new life will grow. It's winter now, so it's slow going, but come springtime, this place will come alive again."

"Not for everything. And that's what I hate the most. I hate the loss. I get the regeneration argument, and I understand bushfires can serve a purpose, but it did nothing to help that poor Tasmanian devil mum and her babies."

"The two you saved are doing well, so Paul tells me."

"It didn't help the butterflies."

Jack pulled me in for a hard hug. "You saved them, remember?"

"Not all of them."

"You did more than anyone else, Lawson. You're not responsible for the bushfire. You are responsible for saving an entire species of butterfly. The Tillman Copper exists because of you."

After a moment of silence, I looked up at him. "Take me home."

He let go of me, pulled on the lapels of my winter coat, and drew me in for a kiss. "My home or your home?" Before I could answer, he added, "You know, it'd save us all this time deciding if you'd just move in with me."

I rolled my eyes, but a smile won out. It wasn't the first time we'd had this discussion, and I doubted it'd be the last. We walked back to his ute. He called Rosemary, who had gone sniffing about, and buckled her in once she'd jumped up onto the back tray. We climbed in, and Jack expertly reversed down the old track. It was much easier now with the lack of trees and shrubs.

"One day, Mr Brighton. One day."

"But not now," he said. I could feel his disappointment in the air between us.

"Are things not perfect enough right now?"

He looked from the road to me. "Yes. But they could be even perfecter."

"Perfecter isn't a word."

"Not yet it isn't, no," he said. "Because you haven't said yes yet. Once you're living with me, it'll be a real word."

I rolled my eyes again but reached out my hand. He slipped his palm into mine and I brought his hand to my lips. "One day."

"I'll hold you to that."

I smiled at him. "I should hope so." We were quite a ways back to town, then I asked, "So, have you thought more on what you'll do for time off?"

He was due to have two weeks annual leave; it was winter and it was the quieter time of the year. "Not really. Might just stay at home, get stuff done around the house. I think Remmy and Nico were looking at doing some work around their house, though last I spoke to them, they weren't sure." Jack sighed. "Unless I could convince my super hot boyfriend to maybe come away with me for a day or two. I know he's busy with his work right now, and he's doing some pretty important things. Not to mention he's finishing up his doctorate externally because of his commitment to research. I haven't asked him yet, though, because I don't want him to say no."

I was smiling at how nervous he was. At how adorable he was. "You should ask him."

His eyes went wide. "Really?"

"Yes. His work might be important, but so is his boyfriend. I doubt he'd say no," I said, playing along. Then I added, "And it helps that butterflies are typically dormant in winter."

Jack's grin was huge. "Yes, that helps."

"Jack?"

"Yeah?"

"You still haven't asked me."

He laughed. "Lawson, come away with me for a day or two, or five, or whatever. We can go wherever you want. Melbourne, to see your family, or to New Zealand for some skiing."

"I don't think skiing is really my thing. Though I'm happy to stay at a chalet, drinking wine and reading books in front of a fire. I can be your official ski bunny."

Jack laughed. "I've never had a ski bunny before."

I lifted his knuckles to my lips for a smiling kiss.

I DID love being at Jack's house. It was peaceful there and felt like home. I did want to live with him, but the sensible part of my brain insisted on not rushing. If this was a permanent thing—and I did think it could be—then there was no need to risk moving in together before we were ready.

And the very last thing I wanted to do was ruin what we had.

Winter had well and truly arrived in Tasmania. The

wind was biting, the clouds hung low, and the sun seemed like it was on half-watt. And I loved it. It meant big coats and scarves, boots and woolly socks. It also meant wood fires and blankets on the sofa, cuddles and sleepy TV, and stews for dinner.

And Jack loved my lamb and dumpling stew. Like "devoured it all and asked when I could make it again" kind of loved it. So while he was chopping wood in the backyard, I set a fresh stew to simmer and made him a cup of tea.

When he came in with his arms full of logs and kindling, his nose was red and his cheeks flushed. He stacked his burden by the wood fire and pulled his beanie off, and my god, he smiled at me in a way that made my heart stutter.

I held up his steaming tea. "I made you a cup."

He took the tea and sipped it gently. "Mmm," he hummed appreciatively. He put the cup on the counter, then encased me in his arms, giving me a hug. It made me hum. "I love it when you hug me like that."

He nudged his nose to my ear. "Like what?"

"Like it feeds your soul."

He chuckled, warm and breathily. "It does." He pulled back and looked into my eyes. "That's exactly what it does."

"I love you, Jack," I said. I'd told him a hundred times in the last six months, and it still gave me a thrill to say it.

He pressed his lips to mine softly. "And I love you." He reached over and lifted the lid on the pot of dinner and peeked inside. "And I love your stew."

It made me laugh. "So, have you given more thought to this holiday we're taking?"

"I'll have to get online and have a look," he said, settling back against me, smiling down at me. "I wasn't expecting you to say yes, actually."

"Well, you go look. I'll finish dinner. My laptop's on the table. Just use it to Google whatever you want."

I set about making dumplings for the stew, and Jack disappeared into the lounge room. Just as I was finishing up adding the balls of dough to the stew, Jack called out. "Uh, Lawson? You got an email."

"Who's it from?"

"I didn't open it."

I slid the casserole dish into the oven. "Well, open it."

I set the timer and washed my hands. I was wiping them on a tea towel when I walked back into the lounge room.

Jack was squinting at my laptop screen. "It's from the Cairns Butterfly Conservatory."

I frowned. "What does it say?"

He held my laptop out. "You read it."

I sat beside him and took my laptop, reading the email.

Dear Mr Gale,

We have followed your work closely, with regards to the Tillman Copper...

I scanned through the rest of the email, then read it again, slower this time.

"Lawson, what is it?"

"I've been invited to assist on a study of the Ulysses butterfly."

Jack blinked. "Is that good?"

"I don't know. It's in Cairns, Far North Queensland, Jack."

I could see the moment it dawned on him. "How long does a study take?"

"It says the initial invitation extends to two weeks."

"Can you leave your work right now on the Tillman?"

I nodded slowly, thoughtfully. "Two weeks is fine. Everything is established, and Warner could supervise..."

Jack frowned. "When would you leave?"

I stared at him. Clearly he'd missed my intention. "Correction, Jack. When would *we* leave is a more pertinent question."

It took him a second, then a smile pulled at his lips. "We?"

I chuckled. "I think I just solved our holiday destination problem. We're not going to the snowfields. We're going to the tropics."

CHAPTER TWO

JACK BRIGHTON

GETTING ORGANISED to go on a ten-day working vacation with Lawson was as funny as it was frightening. To say
he was pedantic was an understatement. He had lists. Lots
of lists. He had lists for his work equipment—which I
understood—but he also had lists for everything else.
Including me.

When we asked Remmy and Nico if they could babysit
Rosemary, or dogsit as it were, for the duration of our trip,
Lawson insisted on giving them a list of foods Rosemary
preferred and desired exercise routines. Mercifully, Remmy
accepted the list seriously, thanking Lawson but smiling
at me.

She found him adorable.

So did I. But the list thing was driving me insane.

I was more of a "pack on the day you leave" kind of guy.

When I told Lawson that, he couldn't speak and his eye
twitched.

We compromised by, for his sake, me packing earlier
than the morning we were to fly out to Melbourne and, for
my sake, not needing a list.

He had work to finish up with Professor Warner Tillman on Friday, and I told him I'd meet him at his place in Launceston. We were flying out to Melbourne on Saturday morning, so it was logical I drop Rosemary off at Remmy's on my way Friday afternoon and meet him at his place in time for dinner.

I let myself into his house. I had a key like he had a key to my house. It made sense, given that we might arrive at each other's houses while the other was at work. Yes, having each other's keys was kind of a big deal, but it felt right. So did having some clothes at his place, and not just a toothbrush, but all toiletries. I had some books of mine on his coffee table, like one of his reference books sat on mine. I liked the fact there were reminders of him in my house, and I really liked the fact there were pieces of me in his.

And I had to admit, I *really* liked the direction our relationship was going.

Which is why I was nervous about the envelope I brought with me, the one I slid onto his kitchen counter. The exact same one that matched the letter addressed to him in a pile of unopened mail near the fruit bowl.

Lawson was an enigma, that was for sure. Insanely particular about some things—such as his lists and his data collation and his appearance—but then there was his messy pile of unopened mail and his ability to run late to almost everything.

Leaving the envelope on the kitchen counter, I took my bags into the bedroom and smiled when I saw his perfectly made bed and, at the foot of it, all his perfectly lined up bags, storage tubs, and research gear. Then I looked into his walk-in closet, and I briefly wondered if he was injured at all when the clothes-bomb went off in there.

Just thinking about him made me smile. And hearing his

car pull up out front made me smile even harder. Well, it wasn't really a car. It was a Land Rover Defender. Yep, that's right. The hire car he bitched and whinged about when he first got here was the exact kind of vehicle he chose to lease. And he loved it.

He came in carrying a heavy bag of something and, looking all flustered and gorgeous, slid it onto his dining table. I stood back and watched him, just for a moment. The winter suited him, being all coated up and wearing a woollen beanie, his cheeks and the tip of his nose were flushed pink. He looked good enough to eat.

He turned to me, sighed, and walked over, greeting me with a kiss. "Hello. Was your trip okay?"

"It was fine."

"And you got Rosemary dropped off okay?"

"Yep."

"Was she sad?"

"Nope. Remmy had made her fresh doggie cookies, and Luca was already showing her his winter garden. They had their heads down in the dirt, tails up in the air, and I barely even got a goodbye."

Lawson smiled, then unwrapped his scarf, pulled off his beanie, and undid his coat. He dumped them all on the dining table and started to rifle through the bag he'd brought inside with him. "Sorry I'm late. I had to organise all my research gear to be collected in the morning. It's getting shipped ahead of us and will be in Cairns when we get there. It's so much easier than trying to take it myself. Then I called into the deli on my way home and grabbed us some dinner. I didn't fancy cooking or going out. Is that okay?"

"What are we having?"

He held up a takeaway container. "Mediterranean vegetable lasagne, greek salad, and a chianti."

"Perfect."

He slid the lasagne onto the kitchen counter when he noticed the envelope I'd left there. He picked it up. "What's this?"

"It's my letter from pathology. I see you haven't opened yours either."

"I got it yesterday," he said quietly. "I thought I'd wait for you."

"And I thought we could open them together."

Lawson nodded. "We could."

He was clearly nervous, and truthfully, so was I. We'd discussed this at length and agreed that full blood tests were a natural step forward for our relationship. He didn't want to use condoms anymore. He said he wanted me and nothing else inside him.

Now, I'd never *not* used protection, ever. But I'd never been in love with someone like I was with him before either. I also couldn't see myself wanting anyone but him. And when he put it like that, about me being the only thing inside him, I couldn't argue.

So we'd gone together to have blood tests, and the results sat, unread, folded in white envelopes. Lawson was still holding mine, nervously licking his lips and turning the letter over in his hand, so I picked up his. "Why are you so nervous?"

"I don't know. Because this can't be undone, and I want this but I'm also equally fine with it if we don't. Don't ever use condoms, that is."

I would have chuckled at how cute he was if he wasn't being so serious. I stood before him, leaned against him until he was backed up against the kitchen counter, and lifted his chin. "Lawson, we've both been tested before and it was fine. This is just a formality, really. A peace of mind."

He looked intently into my eyes. "Jack, please know that whatever the results are, nothing will change how I feel about you."

I kissed him softly. "Same, Lawson. I love you, that won't change."

He finally smiled. "Thank you."

"How about you read mine, and I read yours?"

He frowned for half a second, then nodded. "Okay." But just as I'd slid my finger through the envelope seal, he said, "Wait!"

I froze. "What?"

"Should we eat dinner first?"

I barked out a laugh but quickly realised he was being serious. I knew him well enough to know he needed some time. I took the envelope from his hand and, along with the one I was holding, slid them back onto the kitchen counter. I kissed him again, soft and lingering. "We can worry about that later."

So, we ate our dinner, then ended up on the sofa under a fleecy throw blanket, wine glasses in hand. "I know reverse cycle heating is convenient, but I do miss my wood fire," I mused.

"There's a lot to be said about wearing sweatpants and socks and snuggling with you under a blanket," he said, sipping his wine. He bent his leg and slid his socked foot along my thigh under the blanket.

I chuckled. "True. It is nice."

"It'll almost be a shame to go to Cairns. Though I'm not opposed to seeing you all sweaty, wearing next to nothing."

"You can see that here. Anytime you want."

He laughed and hummed an impatient sound, then without breaking eye contact, he downed the rest of his wine in one mouthful and put his glass on the coffee table.

He stood up and held out his hand. "You shouldn't put explicit imagery in my mind. I have no self-control when it comes to you."

"Explicit imagery? All I said was that you could see me half-naked and sweaty here. You were the one who mentioned the half-naked and sweaty first."

Lawson rolled his eyes. "Your argument is subjective."

I snorted out a laugh, put my wine glass next to his, and stood up. I gripped his jaw and tilted his face up so I could flutter my eyelashes along his cheek. I only did it because it made his breath catch. I waited for his eyelids to slowly open, revealing unfocused eyes. "I'm going to take you to bed, Lawson."

He swallowed hard and nodded. He waited two beats of my heart before sliding his fingers over my hand that was still pressed to his jaw. He squeezed my fingers, and without a word, he led the way to his room.

He walked as far as his bed, then turned to face me. There was worry in his eyes. "What about the test results?"

I opened the top drawer of his bedside table and took out a condom and the small bottle of lube. I threw them onto the bed and kissed him softly. "Not until you're certain."

I could feel the relief roll off him.

I smiled. "Now, I want you naked, on the bed, on your hands and knees."

He let out a slow breath and his pupils blew out. But he did exactly as I asked, and I gave him everything he demanded.

"ARE YOU NERVOUS?"

"No."

"Why aren't you nervous?"

"Because I'm not."

"How can you not be?"

I snorted. We were in the backseat of a cab, having just arrived in Melbourne, on our way to his parents' house. "Lawson, I'm completely fine. You, on the other hand, seem to be very worried. Is that something I should be worried about?"

"No, of course not. It's just that..."

"It's just what?"

"Well, I've not taken anyone home to meet my family before."

Oh. "Are you worried they won't approve of me?"

His eyes went wide, horrified. "Oh, good gracious, no. They'll love you, I'm sure of it."

"Then what's the problem?" But as I asked this question, it dawned on me what the answer was. "You're worried about what they'll see in you."

Lawson opened his mouth, promptly shut it again, then sighed dramatically, and I knew I was right. "You don't understand. I've never been with anyone... I care deeply for in their company. I don't know how to act accordingly. Mackellar and Paterson never had such problems, of course. Their partners are lovely, but they're very... heteronormative. If you know what I mean."

He was so endearing. "Lawson, they know you're gay, right?"

"Yes, of course."

"And you told them we're together?"

His eyebrows knitted. "Yes, you know I have. You've spoken to my mother on the phone."

"Exactly. So you have nothing to hide and nothing to

worry about. I'm not about to grope you in front of your parents. We don't have to hold hands or anything. We can even sit at opposite ends of the house if that's what you're worried about."

He cringed. "Would you be offended?"

"Not at all."

He scrubbed his hands over his face, then patted down his hair. Something I noticed he did when he was nervous or flustered. "Maybe my worries are unfounded. And completely my own. I'm sorry, I shouldn't have said anything."

I took his hand and kissed his palm. "Lawson. I'm sure it'll be fine." The truth was, I had no idea if it would be fine or not. They were, after all, geniuses in their chosen medical fields, and I was, well, not as educated as them. But I loved Lawson, and that was all I had to offer. If that wasn't enough, then that said more about them than it did about me.

Not to say that I didn't hope they would like me and welcome me into their family, given I had every intention of being around for a long time, but if they didn't, then that was that. I wouldn't beg or change who I was.

"Have you met someone's parents before?"

Lawson's question threw me by surprise. "Not since high school. I dated a guy from a different high school and I met his parents, but we were just kids."

"What about when you were at university?"

I shook my head. "I went to uni in Sydney, as you know." We'd talked about all this before. "I never saw anyone seriously enough to bring them back to Hobart to meet my family."

"Will I? Meet your family, that is."

I smiled. "Yes, of course. Well, you've chatted with

April a few times on the phone. She thinks you're lovely. We can drive down to Hobart one weekend, and I can finally take you out on a proper date."

"Proper date?" He frowned. "Are you implying that the dates we've had aren't proper? Because I would take great personal offence to that. That picnic in your backyard is unsurpassable."

I smiled at him. "We might wear suits and eat the very best food."

He sat back in the seat, his worries seemingly forgotten. "You made peanut butter sandwiches and we drank mulled cider under the stars. I'd dare a Michelin-star chef to top that."

The taxi pulled up to a house, a modest but well-kept weatherboard home, and Lawson patted down his hair. "Right then, here we are."

We paid the fare, grabbed all our luggage and by the time I turned to face the house, a woman was standing on the front veranda. She had shoulder-length, grey wavy hair, wore a long flowing skirt and a peasant-style top, and looked like she'd walked straight out of Woodstock. I thought that couldn't possibly be Lawson's mother. I was expecting a well-to-do, straight-backed woman—more like Lawson—not a hippie. But then she extended her arms and cried, "Lawson!"

Lawson grinned at her. "Mum!"

I was stunned. Then she raced down the path and threw her arms around me. "And you must be Jack!"

CHAPTER THREE

I COULDN'T HELP but smile as my mother embraced Jack on the footpath, then dragged him by the arm up to the house.

"No, that's fine," I called out after them. "I'll get our luggage."

Jack gave me a happy, slightly terrified glance over his shoulder as my mum hauled him in through the front door. I grumbled as I towed the two suitcases up the front path, then struggled to get them up the few steps. Thankfully my brother Paterson was soon there, taking Jack's suitcase from me. "Welcome home," he said warmly.

I straightened and smiled. It really was good to see him. "Thank you. I'm glad you're here today."

"Wouldn't have missed it." He put his hand to the front door, but before opening it, he stopped and turned to me. "It's about time we met this Jack fellow I keep hearing about. I'm almost certain he was attached to Mum as she blurred through the house just now."

I ignored the fact my face grew hot. "Yes, well. I've been terribly nervous about bringing him here."

Paterson laughed and clapped his hand gently on my upper arm. "What on earth for? The level of embarrassment that Mum and Dad will put you through is only slightly horrific. She's probably already showing him your baby photos. We probably should go save him."

I sighed, and we pushed our way inside. Paterson and I left the luggage tucked away in the corner of the living room and went in search of Jack. He was, as expected, in the sunroom sandwiched between my mother and father, looking completely overwhelmed. And in that moment, any foolish notion on my behalf of displays of affection in front of my family dissolved. I walked directly to him, positioning myself between Jack and my mother, and slid my arm around his waist, making him take a small step back. I gave my mother a stern look. "Breathing room, please."

Her face, which was positively beaming, softened. She put her hand to my cheek. "Look at you, my sweetest Lawson. Protective and so in love."

A part of me died inside, along with my pride and humility. Someone laughed, and when I looked up, I saw Mackellar sitting at the table, not even attempting to hide her glee at my discomfort. I could probably consider it payback for when she first brought her then-boyfriend, now-husband, James, home to meet our parents. James hid his smile behind his cup of tea. Bree came in from the kitchen, carrying a tray with more cups and a pot of tea, and she gave me a reassuring smile.

Everyone was looking at me, so I patted down my hair and swallowed down my nerves. "Introductions, if you will. Jack Brighton, this is my entire family, all at once. Which I apologise profusely for." I started left to right. "My brother-in-law, James. My sister, Mackellar. My brother, Paterson;

his wife and better half, Bree. My mother, Hyacinth, and my father, Darren. Everyone, this is Jack Brighton."

Gentle hellos echoed around the sunroom, and Jack seemed to take it all in stride. He turned to Mum, who now had her arm linked with his. "Hyacinth? As in *Asparagaceae Hyacinthus*?"

My mother positively glowed. "Ah, a man who knows his genus botanical names! But no, I'm so named after my mother's favourite character from *Watership Down*, Hyzenthlay."

Jack's eyes flashed with something that looked like a memory. "Ah, Richard Adams. I loved that book when I was a kid."

And with that, my mother was besotted with him. With hearts in her eyes, she ushered him to the table. "Come, sit down and tell us about you."

Dad put his hand on my shoulder. "How's life treating you south of the Bass Strait?"

"It's good, Dad."

"And your Tillman Copper? How's the breeding program going? We're all so very proud of you, Lawson."

My chest warmed through. "Thank you. Everything is going splendidly."

We settled around the table for a wonderful lunch of homemade soup and fresh-baked bread and good conversation. I told of all my findings with the Tillman Copper, and everyone asked Jack questions, including him in their conversations, and there was much chatter and laughter. Seeing Jack interact and laugh with my family made me incredibly happy. I hadn't realised how much his acceptance by them, and his acceptance of them, meant to me.

My family wasn't strictly *normal*. I knew that. I'd been

told my entire childhood that we were weird. My mother was never part of the school-mum clique: too alternative for their liking. She didn't dress like them. She certainly didn't think like them. Some days she'd give us the day off school so she could take us into the countryside where we could read in open parks, feeling grass between our toes and the sun on our faces with books in our laps. She told us we'd learn more about life from reading poetry about the earth and love, life and death, than sitting in a classroom all day every day.

She was right. Even as Paterson and Mackellar went on to medical school, they would still take their books to the park, take their shoes off, and spend their days studying in the sunshine. Though I preferred the shade in summer, I found it cleared my mind to read with my back to a tree and my feet in the grass with the occasional butterfly to say hello to.

And growing up, once a week my father would pick a different country and we would search the library on traditional foods and customs. Then we would each help to prepare and cook that country's staples the traditional way and we would discuss their history and culture over the meal. None of my childhood classmates did any such thing, and they quite often reminded me I was not like them. My mother would just hug me and tell me we were the Weasleys in a world of Muggles.

She said there was magic in our individuality. Though over and above everything else, we were taught to be free-thinking and empathetic. And over time, we learned to embrace our individuality.

I know people didn't always agree with my opinion, or my choice of attire, or my sexuality. But everyone in this room loved and accepted me without question. Including Jack. I found myself smiling at him as he told everyone of the two Tasmanian devil joeys I'd saved, and when I felt someone watching me, I turned to see my mum's eyes on me. She was teary and smiling.

"So, tell us, what are your plans for Cairns?" Mackellar asked when Jack's story was done.

Jack answered first. "Well, I imagine Lawson will be busy doing his lepidopterist thing mostly, saving another species no doubt." He put his hand on my knee and squeezed gently. "Though I'm not opposed to spending a few days on the beach or in the national parks. Both, preferably."

"I won't be spending all my time at the conservatory." I gave him a smile. "I'm sure you can spend one day with me in the butterfly house. Then if we go into the Kuranda State Park, you can show me what you do."

The smile he gave me was as warm as the summer sun.

My mother sighed. "Oh, I wish you two could stay a little while longer."

It was then I looked at the clock. "Oh goodness." *Must I be late for everything?* I stood up. "We really should be going."

A few short minutes later, we'd said our goodbyes to my brother and sister and their partners, and Mum and Dad walked us out. My mother had her arm linked through Jack's as they walked ahead of me and Dad. I tried to hear what they talked about, but it was whisper quiet. My dad laughed softly. "Don't worry, Lawson. He's fine. Actually, he's better than fine."

I looked at him and stopped walking. I wasn't aware my father's approval would hold so much weight. "You think?"

He laughed and put his arm around me, walking me forward to where Jack and Mum were standing by the front garden gate. "He makes you happy, Lawson. That's all I need."

As we reached them, my mother put her hands to my face. "My dearest Lawson. I'm so happy for you."

Oh, bother.

"Don't be embarrassed," she said. "Young love is a beautiful thing."

Sweet heavens above. Thankfully the taxi pulled up, and I briefly considered stepping in front of it, if it would mean my mother would stop humiliating me.

Jack and my dad loaded our luggage into the boot. Mum kissed my cheek. "He's wonderful," she whispered.

"I know, Mum."

Before she could respond with anything equally mortifying to Jack, I stuffed him into the taxi and waved my parents off. When we'd reached the end of the block and I could finally breathe, I took Jack's hand. "I apologise for anything my mother may have said to you that you felt was inappropriate or too personal. She has no filter when it comes to, well, most anything."

Jack surprised me by laughing. "Oh my God, Lawson. I love your mother!"

I stared at him. It's quite possible I blinked.

He just laughed some more. "I was expecting some private school headmistress type, but she couldn't be further from that."

"Why would you think she was like a headmistress?"

"Because you were nervous about me meeting her and worried about touching me in front of her."

"Only because she'd be planning our wedding."

"She already is. Well, that and our sex life. She told me

that you were a late bloomer and to be patient with you, if need be."

I stared at him and felt nauseous and horrified. I couldn't speak.

Jack leaned in and whispered in my ear. "I told her patience was not a virtue you were overly fond of in that regard, and that if you had been a late bloomer, you certainly weren't now."

I think I blushed from my hairline to my toes. I let my head fall into my hands. "I'm so sorry," I mumbled.

He kissed my neck, just below my ear before he took my hands from my face and kept our fingers entwined. He gave me a perfectly dimpled smile. "Don't apologise. Your Mum's a hoot. She's so much more than I was expecting. She protests for civil rights and animal rights, she eats organic foods, she's crazy intelligent. And she raised three pretty cool kids."

"You like them?" I asked. "I mean, Paterson and Mackellar?"

"Hell yes. And your dad. You're all so different but very much the same. I don't even know how that works, but seeing you all together makes perfect sense."

I squeezed his hand. "Thank you. It means a lot to me that you like them."

"Of course I like them. How could I not when they each remind me a little of you?"

I chuckled at that, relief and those enigmatic metaphorical butterflies coursed through me.

"Oh, and by the way," Jack added casually. "Your Mum said she wouldn't be too opposed to a wedding in Scottsdale, as long as we promised to spend some time in Melbourne on our way to our honeymoon."

I sank down in my seat. Horrified. Mortified. I squeaked

an apologetic sound.

Jack just laughed and kissed the back of my hand. "It's okay, Lawson. I'm not opposed to it either."

CHAPTER FOUR

JACK

WE BOARDED the plane and settled in for the three and a half-hour flight. I was excited for this trip. Yes, going away for ten days with a boyfriend of just six months was risky, but I had no doubt that Lawson and I were solid.

No doubt.

He was pedantic about so many things, but he was a relaxed traveller. Despite our very first encounter when we met on a plane and he was flustered, this time he was deep breaths and smiles. Well, he read and re-read his research papers, making notes and highlighting, his forehead creasing in thought every now and then. I put on headphones and scrolled the comedy movies until I found something worth watching and let him do his thing.

I understood this was a working vacation for him, and I was perfectly okay with that. I'd never been to Cairns before, and I was looking forward to it. Warmer weather, white sands, and crystal blue oceans, flanked by pristine rainforests. Not to mention the Great Barrier Reef.

After the in-flight meal, I took out the holiday destination brochure from the back of the seat in front of me. I read about the scenic railway, the Skyrail cableway, snorkelling.

"Find anything interesting?" Lawson asked, closing his notepad.

"Sure! Lots to do."

"I wish I could commit to more time with you, but I'm not sure what's expected."

"It's fine. I agreed to come along with you knowing full well that you'd be working. Just promise me two half days out of the ten."

His lips twitched. "I'm certain my schedule will allow that. Anything, in particular, you'd like us to do?"

"I can think of a lot of things," I murmured so only he could hear.

"Any tourist things," he amended, his cheeks pink, "such as sightseeing?"

"Well, more like hiking and snorkelling."

Lawson settled back in his seat. "An outdoorsman. How could I forget?"

"Of course, I'm not opposed to indoor activities. Or even doing indoor activities outdoors."

Lawson flushed a shade of red I'd only seen in nature.

I quirked an eyebrow at him. "Anything I should know?"

He licked his lips. "About what?"

I glanced quickly at the lady on the other side of him. She had earphones on and wasn't paying attention to us. "About doing indoor things outdoors."

Lawson's breath caught, and that was all the reaction I needed. He didn't have to answer.

"Did we by chance book the private courtyard suite?"

THE ROOM WAS a tiki-themed cabana-style room with a huge king-size bed, a spa, a kitchenette, and yes, a private courtyard. The hotel had a gorgeous pool with palm trees, lit with nightlights, and the beach just a block away. I could hear the waves crashing as I opened the glass sliding doors.

But it had been a long day, and Lawson's blinks were getting a little longer, and he did those cute squinty-blinks he did when he was tired.

"Let me order in a late supper," I suggested. "We can have a bath. It's big enough for two. Then bed. You've got an early start tomorrow."

His unpacking seemingly forgotten, he walked over to me and gripped my face, bringing me in for a quick hard kiss. "I'll go run the bath."

Supper eaten, clothes packed away, and all Lawson's research gear accounted for, we slipped into the biggest spa bath ever. He'd even added some bubbles, and it was absurdly comfortable and relaxing. He sat at one end, me at the other, and I picked up one of his feet and started to massage.

He groaned an obscene sound, but closed his eyes and sank lower into the water. He mumbled, "So good."

When I was done with that foot, I collected his other and gave it the same treatment. He was sighing out sex noises. "Didn't realise I was so good at this."

He didn't open his eyes. "You win all the awards." Then he cracked one eyelid. "What did you stop for?"

I snorted and started my ministrations again, kneading my thumb into the arch of his foot. When I'd had enough of that, I lowered his foot back down. "Want me to do your shoulders?"

He lifted one eyelid. "That offer has sexual undertones."

I laughed. "You're too tired for sexual undertones. Turn around, sit between my legs, and I'll massage your shoulders and neck." I held up both pruned hands. "No wicked intent, I promise."

Lawson smiled sleepily but slid over in the tub to settle in between my legs. I kneaded my thumbs into his shoulders, and after about twenty seconds, I think he started to purr. Or snore. It was kinda hard to tell.

I slowly eased him forward, rousing him awake. "Come on. Let's get you to bed."

I pulled the plug and helped him out of the tub. I dried him off the best I could and then did myself before leading him to bed. He was so sleepy and pliant it was cute. I pulled back the covers and climbed into bed after him. I pulled the blanket up over us, settled him into the crook of my arm, and kissed his forehead. There was something to be said about intimacy that wasn't sexual. Sure, I could worship his body with my own for hours on end, and I quite often did, but I could also care for him and make sure he was safe and adored too. Lawson had come into my life so unexpectedly, and I had fallen haphazardly head over heels in love with him.

And as he nuzzled into me, trying to get closer to me even in sleep, I had no doubts he loved me too.

I drifted off to sleep and dreamed of running through fields of long grass chasing butterflies with Lawson, and we were laughing in the sunlight, and then we were the butterflies flittering over pockets of air, weightless and carefree. Then we were fucking and I was buried inside him and he was so warm and wet...

Wait, what?

I jerked awake to find the room lit with the sunrise and Lawson smiling wickedly around my cock.

He was fully dressed, bow tie and all, and I was stark naked and half-asleep but almost ready to come. "What are you doing?" I asked, my voice thick with sleep, rolling my hips for him.

He hummed and pulled off. "You took care of me last night. Now I'm taking care of you." He didn't wait for me to reply, he simply took me into his mouth again and used his hands to fondle my balls and trace my arsehole, then pump me until I couldn't hold back any longer. He moaned when I came, swallowing down everything I gave him.

I was utterly boneless, heavy as lead, and my head was spinning. He appeared above my face, his swollen lips smiling victoriously. "I ordered breakfast for you. It'll be delivered at half seven." He planted a kiss on my lips. "Have a good day." And he was gone.

I smiled at where his face had been and dozed in a sated slumber until room service delivered breakfast.

I SPENT the day walking along the esplanade enjoying the sunshine. It was weird for me to be wearing shorts and a T-shirt in the middle of winter, but it sure was a nice break from the Tasmanian winter we'd left behind. I spent the afternoon by the hotel pool, lazing on a lounge chair, reading, dozing, relaxing. I couldn't remember the last time I'd spent a day doing this little.

It was glorious.

By the time I wandered to our room, I was warmed through like a stone in the sun, slightly sun-kissed, and my skin felt tight from the salt water from the pool. I was surprised to find Lawson there. "Oh, I hadn't realised the time," I said, kissing him soundly. It was almost five. The still-present sun fooled me into thinking it wasn't that late. "Have I ever told you how glad I am that butterflies aren't nocturnal?"

Lawson smiled and kissed me again. "You haven't actually told me that, no."

"Well, I am. It means you spend nights with me and not them."

"Are you jealous of butterflies?"

"Insanely."

He laughed. "How did you spend your day? You look like you spent the day in the sun."

"I did. It was great. Winter in the tropics is just like our summer back home. I walked along the beach, ate fish and chips by the water, and spent the whole afternoon by the pool. Salt water and sunshine. It was lovely." I took his hand and led him to the sofa. "Tell me everything you did today."

"I met Piers Bonfils, director of the Cairns Butterfly Conservatory. He's the man who emailed me, inviting me to come."

"What's he like?"

"He has contributed to the *Annales de la Société Entomologique de France*, so yes, he's quite renowned. He was on the Committee of the Association of Lepidoptera in France before he came to Australia."

Lawson sounded impressed, and I figured this guy's resumé was something to be respected.

"What kind of team does he have?"

Lawson smiled and squeezed my hand. "Can we talk over dinner? I'll tell you everything, but I'm starving. I didn't eat lunch today."

"Oh, of course. Room service or dinner out? Which would you prefer?"

"I'm sure we can find a café on the esplanade."

"Perfect. Let me grab a quick shower, just to wash the salt water off me. I feel a bit sticky."

Lawson's right eyebrow flickered up as did the corner of his mouth. "Or you could leave it so I can taste it later."

I laughed. "Or we could take a night swim together after dinner? Then afterwards you can taste me as much as you want."

He gave me an insufferable sigh and a smirk. "If I must."

A quick two-minute shower later and I came out of the cubicle to find Lawson at the vanity. He sprayed deodorant under his arms, then washed his face. "I'll shower after our swim," he said, slipping a clean shirt on.

"What? No bow tie?"

"No time. I'm starving. Hurry up and get dressed."

I threw on the closest outfit I could find and pulled the door shut behind us. I knew Lawson well enough to know that he was grumpy if he didn't eat. We got to the footpath and I pointed to the quickest route to the esplanade. "This way."

We found a little café on the waterfront. Lawson ordered the grilled chicken salad and then proceeded to eat most of the fries off my plate. I laughed at him. "Want half my burger too?"

He sat back and patted his belly. "Not now."

"So tell me, what's up with the Ulysses butterfly, and why did the gorgeous Lawson Gale need to cross the country for it? I mean, I do understand you are the best lepidopterist there is, but..."

He ignored my compliment. "The Ulysses isn't breeding successfully."

I thought about that for a moment. "So you came all this way to put them in the mood?"

He chuckled. "Kind of. Well, they are breeding, but it's not viable."

"Did you try serenading them? Dinner first? No wait, tell them all they're serial killers and dazzle them with your intelligence. Totally worked for me."

Lawson laughed. "It did. However, I don't think butterflies and you have that much in common."

I feigned offence. "I'll have you know, I give the best butterfly kisses."

He hummed, and happiness seemed to radiate from him. "You certainly do."

"So, if I were a butterfly, what breed would I be?"

"Hmm." Lawson tilted his head and considered this. "You're more of a dragonfly. The *Calopteryx virgo* to be exact. Strikingly beautiful."

I smiled at that. "But you're a butterfly?"

"Probably."

"You are," I confirmed. "So why can't I be the same as you?"

"Do you need to be the same as me?"

"Yes. How can we be compatible if we're not?"

He gave me a fond smile. "Fair enough. If you were a butterfly, you'd be a White Dragontail."

"Why?"

His eyes never left mine. "Well, again, incomparable beauty, transparent wings, and they usually copulate for hours at a time."

I barked out a laugh. "Is that right?"

"Absolutely." He had that playful, amused spark in his eyes. "You said, rather adamantly, that I would be a butterfly."

"Yes. It's true. Now, I'm not up to date on their copulation habits, but metaphorically speaking, you come across as an unassuming, shy guy, but you really do have wings. You just don't show them to many people."

He looked at me like he couldn't tear his eyes away. He swallowed hard.

I gave him a smile. "When you were explaining to me what imago was, I kept thinking it was just like you. You'd shown me your true self, and Lawson, it was a remarkable sight."

His nostrils flared, his eyes were dark with lust, and he swallowed again. "Jack, you need to take me back to our room. Now."

I looked around for our waitress and put my hand up to get her attention. "Bill, please."

WHEN WE LEFT THE CAFÉ, Lawson slipped his hand into mine. We hadn't really been anywhere together that warranted holding hands. If we walked down the street in Scottsdale, one of us was usually holding a bag of produce or Rosemary's leash. When we were in Launceston, we were usually at his place or at professor Tillman's butterfly house. Sure, we went out for dinner occasionally, but we'd park close to the restaurant. We rarely walked anywhere far enough to hold hands.

He squeezed my fingers. "Is this okay?"

"It's more than okay."

He walked with a skip in his step back to the hotel, and when we passed the pool, I pointed to it. "Wanna take a dip?"

"After."

"After what?"

He fit the key into the lock and pushed the door open. "After what you're about to do to me."

He walked in first, unbuttoning his shirt as he went. He tossed it onto the floor and kept walking into the bedroom. He stopped in the doorway, looked right at me while he undid the button and zipper on his pants. "Waiting for something?"

Fucking hell.

I stepped inside and locked the door behind me just in time to see his pants being flung to the floor.

"I'm starting without you," he said, his voice tight.

When I got to the bedroom door, I found him on the bed, on his back with his knees bent. His right hand gripped his cock, his left rubbed over his hole. A bottle of lube lay next to him on the bed.

"Lawson," I breathed his name.

He slipped a finger inside himself. "Jack, you're not naked and you're not inside me."

I pulled my shirt over my head and toed out of my shoes. I pulled my socks off and slid my shorts over my hips. I was already hard. Seeing him laid out before me like that, offering himself to me, turned me on like nothing else could.

I gave myself a few strokes but then had to pull on my balls to stave off my orgasm. Jesus. I wasn't going to last at this rate.

Lawson writhed on the bed, jerked himself, and added another finger to his slicked hole. "Jack," he bit out. "You're still not inside me."

I knelt on the bed and took the foil packet he'd put near the lube. I rolled the condom down my length and Lawson moaned. I knew if I left it a moment longer, that filthy mouth of his would—

"Jack, I need your cock in me when I come. If you don't fuck me soon—"

And there it was.

"Take your hand away," I ordered and moved into position between his thighs.

He gripped the backs of his knees and I pressed the blunt head of my cock to his hole. "Just fucking do it," he ground out.

I pushed into him, in one full thrust.

His eyes went wide, his jaw bulged, and he gritted his teeth.

I knew he could take it. And not just take it but love every second. "Is that what you want?"

He nodded and breathed, his body relaxing. "God yes." I slowly rocked my hips, giving him time to adjust. "Fuck me, Jack. Make me yours."

God, his words were fuel to a fire I was trying to contain.

I couldn't help it, I couldn't stop. I slammed into him, deeper than I'd ever been, and his mouth fell open; his neck corded. He gasped and moaned. "Yes, like that."

Leaning back on my haunches, I took his cock in my hand and pumped him while I fucked his arse. Lawson put both his hands on his head, pulled at his hair, and shook his head. Precome was leaking from his slit, and he bucked his hips. He was hard and close to coming, so close.

"You like being filled with my cock," I grated out. "And soon it'll just be me, nothing else. And when I come, you'll feel it."

Lawson's whole body jerked, his arse tightened around me, and his cock swelled in my hand before spilling come onto his belly.

He was glorious.

When he sagged beneath me, I let go of his spent dick and leaned over him so I could kiss him. And I kept kissing him. What had started out as hard and fast fucking was now slow-and-sweet lovemaking.

Lawson fisted my hair and rolled his hips, taking every inch of me in every unhurried thrust. He broke our kiss but spoke against my lips. "I can't wait to have your come inside me."

And that was all it took.

My orgasm exploded at the base of my spine and bloomed through my whole body. Pleasure burned in my veins, and Lawson held onto me: he wrapped his legs and arms around me as I filled the condom inside him.

I didn't know if I passed out, but I kind of came to with Lawson gently stroking the hair from my forehead and planting soft kisses to my nose. We were a sticky mess but neither of us seemed too keen to move. He hummed contentedly. "Hmm, how about I get a cloth to clean us up, then we go for that swim?"

I smiled at him. "How about you stay right here, and I get us the cloth, then we go for that swim."

A slow spreading smile covered his face. "Okay."

I kissed his lips and slid out of bed. I disposed of the condom, grabbed a washcloth, and wet it before cleaning him up. I threw his swimming trunks onto the bed and pulled on my boardies, then we headed out to the pool.

"Oh," I said on our way out. "I forgot about the courtyard."

"What about the courtyard?"

"Doing indoor activities outdoors, remember?"

Lawson put his hand on the pool fence gate and raised one eyebrow at me. "Pool's empty?"

I laughed. "Maybe the pool's a little too public. I don't

fancy having a criminal record for indecent exposure, if you know what I mean. I think the courtyard might be more private, yet still outdoors."

He tilted his head in that adorable way he did when considering all the facts presented to him. "Good call." He swung the gate open, threw his towel onto a pool chair, and dived cleanly into the water.

He surfaced, glistening wet and smooth, looked up at me, and grinned. "Getting in, Jack? Or do you intend to stand there and stare at me all night?"

"I dunno," I answered, looking right at him. "The view's pretty good from here."

He laughed and smoothed back his dripping wet hair. "I'm sure it is. But the *view*, if that's what we're calling me, is interactive in the water."

I threw my towel next to his and dove, not as gracefully as him I'm sure, into the water. I came up close enough to him, but as soon as I found my feet, he launched himself at me. He threw his arms around my neck and kissed me, and I slipped my hands around his back.

I had no idea that a wet-Lawson was such a hot-Lawson. He broke away with a smirk. "I'm going to do some laps. Care to join me?"

I shook my head slowly. "You go ahead. I'd much rather just enjoy the view."

So he turned and glided through the water with strong and languid strokes, and I stayed with my back to the end of the pool, watching him.

Until I got bored with that. And when he swam up to touch the end of the pool, I pounced on him. He came up spluttering out a laugh. "What was that for?"

"I prefer the interactive view."

He folded his legs around my hips, locking his feet

behind my back, his arms wound around my neck. "Ever kissed anyone underwater?"

I shook my head. "No."

"Neither have I."

I laughed, but apparently that was not the right response. He gave me his stern face, his no-nonsense, you-might-be-bigger-than-me-but-I'm-the-one-in-charge face. "Jack, take me to the deep end and kiss me underwater."

Have I ever mentioned I'm a sucker for a bossy power bottom? "Your wish. My command."

CHAPTER FIVE

LAWSON

PIERS BONFILS WAS A PASSIONATE FRENCHMAN. Handsome, late fifties, with eyes the same colour as his dark-grey hair, and a lighter grey goatee. He was tanned and fit and walked with a fluid grace that was borne of his confidence and ego.

I liked him. He spoke his mind, a trait I admired in anyone, and had the intellect to back up his arguments. But he also listened with an open mind, never afraid to learn. And that was a rarity, especially in my field.

He had met my old boss from Melbourne, Professor Asterly, a few times, and although he appreciated the man's input to lepidoptery, he never much liked the way he played the political game to further his career.

"Asterly can deny it all he likes," Piers said, his accent thick, "but the truth is, he disliked me because of who I choose to bed. Nothing to do with my career. I assume he's the same with you?"

I blinked in surprise. We were having lunch in his office, not discussing our private lives in a bar or something. "I uh. Um."

Piers smiled knowingly at me. "It's fine with me, Lawson. I will never hide the fact I'm gay. Neither do you. I thought you would understand."

This was not a conversation I was strictly comfortable having. "I am, gay, that is, and I do understand. Only I separate my personal life from my professional life. I would never want details of Professor Asterly's sexual habits, and I expect the same courtesy."

He smiled as though I charmed him. "Ah, we are of different generations, young Lawson. You are of an age where it is accepted and no one bothers you, you know? But I had to fight for it and not hide who I was, even if it could cost me my job. Asterly always thought he was better than me for this reason. The wolves were always at my door, and he was given research grants as rewards."

"I was unaware of this," I said, pushing my water away. "Though I would hardly be surprised. He never warmed to me. I assumed it was because I spoke my mind and refused to pander to everything he said."

Piers laughed. "This is why Professor Tillman sought you out!"

"Well, yes. Professor Asterly was not happy."

He threw his hands up and said some rather choice words in French. I knew enough to piece together what he meant. But he offered me a smile. "Serves him right."

I folded my sandwich wrapper neatly in half, then half again, pressing it down flat. Piers was watching me with a smile. "So tell me, Lawson. What is your expert opinion thus far on the Ulysses?"

"I agree with your findings. Everything you list is accurate, and there are no discrepancies in your data."

He nodded slowly. "I should hope not."

"It would be counterproductive of me to assume your

figures and percentages are correct without checking for myself. If I took your data as gospel and there was an error, I'd never find the inconsistency."

"True."

"Given the data is sound, we need to determine external factors, as I'm sure you're very aware."

Piers smiled and scrunched up his sandwich wrapper. "Yes."

"The fact the butterflies can breed and are willing is encouraging. Why the caterpillar survives but the butterfly dies is the concern."

"Your first thought?"

"External factors, such as climate and diet, would be my first guess. Given the butterfly house is and has been a constant temperature and humidity for years without incident before now gives me reason to lean toward diet."

"Ah, but nothing has changed in their diet."

"With all due respect, Professor Bonfils, that's where you're wrong. Because something *has* changed. Those butterflies are telling us something has changed. We just need to figure out what it is."

I GOT BACK to the hotel room feeling disgruntled and irritated. Though Jack was there with a welcoming smile and a hug that held healing qualities. I could feel my worries dissipate in the few seconds he held me in his strong, warm arms.

"You've had a crap day," he stated. He could tell. I nodded against his chest. "Tell me about it."

"Are you sure?" I asked, still with my face pressed into

his shirt. "Because I feel the need to rant and I fear it will be misdirected at you."

I could hear the quiet rumble of his laughter through his chest. "You ranting in all your passionate glory is one of my favourite things."

I finally smiled.

"Let me guess," Jack said. "Bonfils is an idiot."

I sighed. "Well, not exactly. He just has idiotic views."

Jack's whole body vibrated when he chuckled. He tightened his arms around me. "What did he say?"

"Normally he's very receptive and open to ideas, but he's refusing to see reason. I understand he's frustrated and upset with what's happening to the Ulysses, but"—I pulled back a little so I could look up at his face—"how can someone who has dedicated his career to the betterment of lepidoptery be so ignorant to the plight of his very cause?"

"How so?"

I huffed out a sigh. "The Ulysses is in decline. The breeding program is failing, and he is unwilling to believe external environmental factors are at play. 'Nothing has changed.'" I imitated the Professor's accent. Then I growled out my frustration. "He's a scientist. How can a scientist ignore facts? I told him he was wrong."

Jack smiled. "Of course you did."

"Something has changed. Those butterflies are telling us something has changed, but he won't listen to them."

"How does one listen to a butterfly?" Jack wasn't placating me. He was serious, as though he really wanted to know the answer.

"We watch. We learn. We study their habits, movements, habitat. The butterfly house is a controlled environment, and for many years, it's worked exceptionally well."

"Is it the air quality?"

I smiled. "I've tested that. The air filtration system is well maintained and there have been no recent changes. The humidity is perfect."

Jack frowned. "Then it has to be diet. If their habitat hasn't changed, the air and humidity are fine, then it has to be diet."

I clawed my face. "Oh my God, Jack, if you can see that and I can see that, why can't he?"

"You've suggested this?"

"I told him it had to be the likely contributing factor."

"And he refutes it?"

"He simply claims it can't be because nothing has changed."

"Well, that's stupid."

Despite my frustrations, I laughed. "I may have said that also."

Jack put his hands on the tops of my arms. "Would you like a glass of wine?"

"I would love one." I leaned up and kissed his lips. "Then you can tell me what you did today."

I collapsed onto the sofa, feeling better already, and Jack walked back from the kitchenette with a glass of wine in each hand. He handed me one and sat side-on to me with one leg folded up underneath him, giving me his undivided attention. "Sure you don't want to vent some more?"

I sipped my wine and shook my head. "No. I want to hear all about your day."

"Well, I walked the esplanade again, though I'm not too keen on going in the ocean. There are warning signs listing all the things that bite in there, so I think I'll stick with the pool. I did some laps, had a lunch of fresh seafood."

"And you're bored," I deduced.

He gave me a smile. "A little. I'm used to being busy all

the time, and yesterday it was great to be lazy, but by lunchtime I was itching to do something constructive."

"I'm sorry."

"What for?"

"It's because of me we're spending your holiday time up here, and I'm busy working. That's not fair on you."

"I like being here with you. And anyway, I was thinking of heading up to the national parks office tomorrow and introducing myself. You know, one park ranger to another."

"Is there some kind of code you guys go by?"

He laughed and sipped his wine. "Only that we're smarter than the av-er-age bear." His impersonation of Yogi Bear was disturbingly good.

I couldn't help but laugh. "Do all park rangers make Yogi Bear jokes?"

He grinned and put on his Yogi voice again. "Ah, that's Mr Ranger, sir, to you, Boo-Boo."

It really wasn't that funny, but all I could do was laugh. If that was his intent—to make me happy after my frustrating day—it sure worked.

"What did you feel like for dinner?" he asked eventually.

"What? No pic-a-nic baskets?"

He chuckled warmly. "A picnic on the beach is a great idea."

So, half an hour later, I was changed into shorts and a T-shirt, and Jack was carrying a bag from the supermarket. Tonight we feasted on roast chicken, fresh baked bread, marinated artichokes, and olives. And wine, of course. We found a quiet place on the sand and sat down, facing the beautiful Pacific Ocean just as the sun had almost disappeared behind us. "We should have brought a blanket," Jack mused.

"No. This is perfect."

He held out a plastic cup we'd bought from the super-market and grinned. "Not exactly high class."

I chuckled. "This is better than high class. This is us."

He opened the wine and poured some into my cup, then into his own. He held his plastic cup up to mine and repeated my words back to me. "This is us."

The night was dark, but the esplanade was lit well enough that we were hidden by night from most of the passers-by. We ate some dinner, using our fingers, feeding each other, and laughing at the mess we'd made of ourselves. He was so much fun, and I hated the idea of him being bored on his own during the day.

"Come with me tomorrow," I said, "to the butterfly conservatory. I have one or two things that need attending in the morning then in the afternoon we can go up to the park. How does that sound?"

Jack grinned in the faint light of the esplanade. "Sounds perfect."

THE LOOK on Jack's face as he walked into the butterfly conservatory was one I'd never forget. His eyes were wide with wonder, identical to his smile. "Oh my God, Lawson. This is incredible."

And it was. I agreed.

The butterfly conservatory wasn't just a lab or a butterfly house where we kept pupas and chrysalises. There was a huge atrium with a climate-controlled rainforest where butterflies were free to flutter and roam as they would in the wild. It truly was an amazing setup and one I could only hope to achieve back in Tasmania.

I'd explained procedure and what not to do, and Jack's excitement was adorable and contagious. "And we can go inside it?" Jack asked.

I chuckled and opened the door. "Yes, of course."

Once inside, we walked over the wooden bridge and moved to the centre near the water feature. "Okay, just lift your arms out and stand still," I urged him. I took a half-cut orange from a feeder and put it in the palm of his hand.

"What are you doing?"

"Just wait."

He did as I instructed. "Oh my God," Jack squeaked as a Ulysses butterfly flittered over to him, landing on his chest, then another on his shoulder. "What are they doing?"

"Be careful. They're the last two breeding pair left here."

He remained stock still, but his gaze shot to mine. "Last?"

I nodded slowly. "Unfortunately, yes."

"I didn't realise it was so dire. When you said there was a breeding problem..."

"It's more of a longevity issue. They breed just fine. But they're dying soon after imago."

Jack frowned and watched the butterfly for a quiet moment. "My God, it's beautiful." He looked at the butterfly now on the orange in his hand. "It's huge. I wasn't expecting it to be so big!"

"They like you," I said with a laugh. "Well, they like your shirt."

He shot me a look. "You told me to wear this one today."

"Because it's blue. They're attracted to the colour blue."

A green birdwing butterfly landed on his forearm. He made a funny face that was part comical, part awe. "Holy shit, it's big. I can feel its feet, and it tickles."

"He's tasting you," I explained. Then I hummed. "I have to say. I've never been jealous of a butterfly before."

Jack laughed, and I put my hand up to his outstretched arm, trying to tempt the butterfly onto my fingers. We both stood breathless, watching as the butterfly flittered from him to me and back to him. When our gazes locked again, we both smiled at what had just passed between us. It was a strangely private moment. Quiet and reverent. Personal.

Then Jack looked over my shoulder to something behind me. "There's a man watching us."

"Oh?" My first thought was that someone might not appreciate two men being caught in a questionable moment. "Is he angry?"

Jack frowned. "No. Sad."

I turned around then to find Professor Bonfils. "Oh, good morning, Professor," I said, relief washing through me. "I hope you don't mind I brought Jack in this morning. I wanted to show him the reason we're in North Queensland and why he's not skiing in New Zealand."

It took a moment for him to smile, which was an odd reaction.

So I quickly added, "I can assure you I've taken every precaution with quarantine."

Piers held his hand up as a peace offering. "It's fine, Lawson." Then he nodded to Jack. "Professor Piers Bonfils. It's a pleasure to meet you. Is it Jack? I'd like to say I've heard all about you, but I haven't. Lawson didn't mention he had a travel companion."

I didn't care much for the professor's tone but Jack smiled good-naturedly. "Jack Brighton. I would shake your hand, but Lawson told me not to move. And that's okay about me being a surprise; I don't expect Lawson to talk about me at work."

I frowned. "Well no. I don't cross-contaminate my personal and professional lives."

Jack appeared as if he was trying not to laugh, though I couldn't understand why. So I added, "And Jack is more to me than a travel companion."

Piers gave me a tight smile. His accent was particularly thick when he said, "I could see that." Then his face softened, as though he'd remembered his manners. "I was watching when the butterflies first landed on you." He turned his attention to Jack and the two butterflies still on his shirt. "Magnificent creatures, no?"

Jack gave him one of his disarming smiles, dimples and all. "They're remarkable."

Piers' peculiar tension seemed to dissipate as he told Jack about this particular Ulysses, and when there was a brief pause in the conversation, I interrupted. "If you don't mind, Professor, I'm just going to check the water samples." I gave Jack an apologetic glance as I left them to talk.

I entered the lab area and quickly set about checking the samples I'd taken on day one and day two. I'd taken petri dish swabs to see if the issue was bacterial, and I had sent samples to the CSIRO for analysis. I was doing everything that Piers had already done, but I had to see the data for myself.

All pH levels were fine. All bacteria was fine and well within the healthy range.

With a final check of emails, I printed off the CSIRO soil report and read through their findings. All readings were normal. Potassium levels were toward the higher range of normal, but nothing stood out as problematic.

It was frustrating, but by process of elimination, it was still something. If it wasn't the air or the water affecting the Ulysses, it had to be diet.

I was more convinced.

Piers appeared at my side, startling me. "Oh!"

He gave me a sad smile, then nodded to the report in my hand. "Find anything new?"

"No. Nothing really."

He nodded slowly. He appeared uncomfortable or distracted.

"Everything okay? Where's Jack?"

Piers looked back to the atrium. "Oh, he's still with the butterflies. He's quite fascinated."

I smiled.

Piers studied me a moment. "That look on your face. You love him."

"That's hardly professional and quite frankly not up for discussion."

He waved me off. "Oh, Lawson. It's perfectly fine. Don't be embarrassed. If anything, I'm envious."

"Of my relationship with Jack?"

He bobbed his head in a so-so manner. "More so his relationship with you."

Oh.

"*Oh.*"

He laughed, embarrassed, and shook his head. "It was foolish of me to think... Anyway, he's a very lucky man."

Oh dear. This was terribly embarrassing. "He is a lucky man. As am I. But if you invited me here on the proviso or the assumption that you and I would be compatible... in that manner, you were quite incorrect."

"Not entirely," he said. He looked properly abashed, and I found myself forgiving him.

"Then why *am* I here?"

"For your intellect, to see what I cannot," Piers answered. "You have a proven track record to examine and process. Though you've spent three days repeating data analysis that I assured you was correct. Now you're leaving today to do tourist sightseeing. You keep saying it's the diet, but it cannot be."

Okay, so maybe he wasn't completely forgiven. Piers' passion and temper were not mutually exclusive, and I was only tolerant of so much. "Professor Bonfils, the reason I am here at your request is to help determine possible causes of the decline in the Ulysses. I'm not here to agree with you. If you want someone to pat you on the back and tell you you've done all you can do, then you chose the wrong person. I'm here to help you save this species. If you'd rather I left, tell me now and I'll go. I don't want to waste your time. But I can tell you right now, this butterfly is dying. If you'd rather see it face extinction than admit you could have done more, then I'll have no part of it. If you want to help me help you, then respectfully, sir, take your head out of your arse and help me."

He did his angry-Frenchman-hand-waving thing. "I think I can see why Professor Asterly doesn't like you."

"I don't care what Asterly thinks of me. I don't care what you think of me. I'm not here to be liked, Professor. I'm here to do a job."

His eyes flashed with defiance and possibly amusement. "Despite my best efforts to the contrary, I do like you."

"Thank you. And I respect the work you've done here. It is incredible, and I'm not disparaging your life's work. Quite the opposite, actually. But we need plans and we need them actioned. I'm only here for a limited time."

"Well, about that," Bonfils replied cautiously. "I told you my interests in you being here were only partially personal. If I were to offer you a position here, full-time, to work as co-lead, would you be interested?"

CHAPTER SIX

JACK

LAWSON WAS quiet on the drive to the Kuranda National Park. Granted, it was just around the corner, but he spent the entire time in the car either frowning or scowling, chewing on his bottom lip.

"Everything okay?"

"Hmm?" He looked surprised I'd spoken. "Sorry, I was a million miles away."

I drove the car into a spot in the tourist parking lot. I shut the engine off and looked at him. "I asked if everything was okay?"

"Oh, yes. Well, not really."

"What's going through that brilliant mind of yours, Lawson? Is it the butterflies? Or something else?"

He swallowed hard and shook his head. "It's nothing. Let's go. I'm quite excited to be here."

I looked out the windscreen to where the sign to the Kuranda National Park greeted us. Something was bothering him, but if he needed time to process, then I would give him that. "I'm excited too! We could spend days here, and given we have half a day, we better get moving."

We paid our entry fee and opted for the guided tour, which was an amphibious vehicle that took us into the rainforest floor, exploring the amazing trees and ferns, all the tropical and citrus fruits, then onto the river where we could explore the rainforest from the water. It was incredible, but I really wanted to spend time with Lawson, just us. I wanted to see him experience this rainforest, this new environment, and watch his every reaction.

After the guided tour, we took the Skyrail up to the top of the mountain so we could walk back down, just the two of us.

And I wasn't disappointed.

I could practically hear his mind turning, his love for learning new things shone in his eyes. I mean the rainforest was incredible: damp paths underfoot, dense green foliage, tall trees, and a whole symphony of sounds.

"It's an extraordinary place, isn't it?" I couldn't keep the wonder from my tone.

"Yes, quite," he replied, stopping to look up at the canopy of a particular tree. "Very different from your parks in Tasmania."

"Well, on the west coast of Tassie, we have rainforests similar but not tropical like this. I'll have to take you to the Franklin-Gordon Wild Rivers National Park. Now *that* is something to see." I reached over and put my hand on the trunk of the tree he was looking at. "Wanna know what this is called?"

"Sure."

I grinned. "It's the *Idiospermum australiense* or the Idiot Fruit."

He gave me a disbelieving look. "You're joking?"

"No, I'm not joking! The fruit seed is highly poisonous. No birds or animals will touch it."

"Except for the idiot it was undoubtedly named after."

I laughed. "Probably."

He gave me a smile that didn't quite sit right.

I had planned to give him time, but maybe he needed some prompting. I debated not saying anything, but I hated the fact he was miserable. "Lawson, did Professor Bonfils say something to upset you?"

His gaze shot to mine, and the look on his face told me all I needed to know. He blinked nervously. "Why do you say that?"

"Because you're an open book. I thought it might have just been the butterflies, but that's not it. Something's been bothering you since we left the conservatory this morning. I figured it was him because he went off to speak to you, and you've been quiet since."

"Oh." He chewed on his bottom lip and stared off into the forest.

"Lawson, is it the fact he's attracted to you?"

His eyes bugged out and his mouth fell open, which would've been funny if he didn't go a little pale. "I never encouraged... I didn't know..."

I pulled him against me and hugged him, and chuckling, I kissed the side of his head. "I know. But it was pretty clear from the moment he saw you with me that he was disappointed."

The truth was, Lawson was oblivious to the reactions of most people around him. It would have been obvious to most people that Piers found Lawson attractive, but just not obvious to Lawson.

"I'm sorry," he mumbled.

I pulled back, keeping my hands on his arms. "What on earth for? You've nothing to apologise for."

He sighed and his frown deepened. "He told me he was

jealous that I had a friend such as you. I told him, indisputably, you were more than just a friend, and if his intentions in asking me to come here were romantically inclined, he was very mistaken."

I tried not to smile, but I lifted his chin so he'd look at me. I pecked my lips to his. "Thank you. Though I had no doubt. I trust you, Lawson. Implicitly."

The corner of his lip pulled down. "There's something else."

A cold trickle of dread seeped into my chest. "What's that?"

"I wasn't going to say anything, but I can't... I won't keep secrets from you."

The trickle became a pool.

"He's asked me to join his team. Permanently."

"What?"

"Professor Bonfils has officially requested I join his team on a permanent basis here, in far north Queensland."

I blinked. "Oh. What did you say?"

"Nothing. Before I could answer, he told me to think about it."

"What about your Tillman Copper?"

"Exactly. My work there is very important. I won't leave my own team." He stared into my eyes. "I don't want to leave you, either. You're very important too."

Relief coursed through me. I couldn't deny it. He slipped his hand into mine and gently pulled me to keep walking. "Come on. We better get heading back." He lifted my hand to his lips and kissed my knuckles. "You can tell me more botanical names on the way."

———

I FELT KINDA DETACHED after Lawson told me that he'd been offered a job here. I was pissed off and scared too because I'd just found the most incredible man, and I could see myself with him forever. In Tasmania. Where we lived. I mean, we didn't live together, per se, but it was only a matter of time. We both knew that.

Or had I assumed that? Were we even on the same page? I thought we were, but now I wasn't sure.

When we got back to the information centre, I was still talking about the *Epiphytes*. They were an amazing plant, in particular, the *Drynaria rigidula* and the Northern Elkhorn. And it was easier for me to keep talking about the ecosystem of plants rather than think about Lawson leaving.

"Well, you certainly know what you're talking about," a woman said. She wore a park uniform, her blonde hair in a ponytail, and a high-wattage smile.

"Oh, hi. Yes, flora and fauna. It's what I do," I said, extending my hand out to her. "Jack Brighton's my name."

"Cassie O'Hearn." She had a firm handshake, and I liked her immediately.

"Lawson Gale." Lawson introduced himself politely. "Jack works for Parks and Wildlife in Tasmania."

"And Lawson's here on a professional invitation from the butterfly conservatory." Then I added, "So, technically, flora and fauna is what *we* do."

Cassie's eyes lit up. "Excellent!

"Maybe you can tell Lawson about the *Dendrocnide moroide*," I suggested to her. "Because he thinks I'm making it up."

Lawson rolled his eyes. "I believe him about the idiot fruit because... well, I don't doubt some idiot ate it and died after being told not to eat it. But a tree that has glass on the leaves?" He gave me a doubtful look. "I'm not gullible."

Cassie laughed. "The Stinging Tree. Rest assured it's very real, and I don't recommend you go near it."

Lawson frowned at her. "He wasn't pulling my leg?"

Cassie shook her head with a smile. "No. The leaves may look harmless, but they're covered with microscopic hairs made of mineral silica: the chief constituent of glass. If you brush against the hair-like tips, they break off and embed in the skin and release a poison irritant. The sting's effect is severe and lasts for months."

Lawson made a face. "That's what Jack said. I'm starting to see why most tourists believe almost everything in Australia is trying to kill you."

She laughed again. "So, you're here from Tasmania?" she asked, looking at me this time. "That's pretty cool. I help look after the Tasmanian devils here. We have a breeding pair, and the newest pups are a handful."

"Oh, can I see them?" Lawson asked excitedly.

Cassie beamed. "Sure!"

We followed Cassie out into the wildlife park, and as we walked to the enclosure, I told her how Lawson had almost died when he saved two joeys from the bushfire. She stopped at the enclosure fence so she could hug him. The look on his face was priceless.

Cassie laughed and looked to a particular spot in the enclosure. "Over there," she said.

The devils were out of the den. Given the late afternoon, it wasn't too surprising. Lawson put his hand on my arm. "Look, Jack, there they are!"

I put my hand on his lower back. "They're bigger than the ones you saved."

"They might be this big by now," he said wistfully, not taking his eyes off the playful joeys.

If Cassie had any problem with mine and Lawson's

displays of affection, even as passive as they were—a gentle touch, a reassuring hand—she certainly didn't let on. In fact, we chatted as we watched the devils rumble and tackle each other.

Just then, another staff member joined us. He introduced himself as Gary, and Cassie explained further, "Gary's one of our vegetation experts." Then she nodded to me. "Jack here's with the Tassie Parks and Wildlife."

Gary's eyes widened, as did his smile. "How're ya finding it up here?"

"It's beautiful."

"Sure is," he agreed. "How long you stayin' for?"

"Another week." I introduced Lawson and mentioned his work with the conservatory. "He has a week to find out what's affecting the Ulysses, save the species, and ensure the entomological ecosystem remains in balance."

Gary and Cassie laughed. Lawson rolled his eyes. "It's hardly that exciting."

"That's a pretty remarkable job," Cassie said.

"It is a remarkable job," I agreed.

"It's one I should get back to," Lawson said, glancing at his watch. "I told the professor I'd be back before he leaves for the evening."

"Ah, how is Professor Piers going?" Gary asked.

"You know him?" Lawson asked.

Gary nodded. "I deal with him a bit. We supply organic fruit and plants for his butterflies."

"Oh, of course," Lawson said. "Piers is okay. He's very passionate about his work. And I'd imagine he won't be too pleased if I'm late."

I took our cue. "Yes, we should be going. Thank you, Cassie, for the private tour."

"Pleasure," she said cheerfully.

Gary put his hand out. "Hey, if you're looking for something to do during the day, I run guided walking tours. Not many people find the biodiversity of our flora as exciting as me, but you might like it."

"I'd love it!" I agreed. "And actually, I have a few hours to spare."

"Excellent!"

We said our goodbyes, and I was quite excited about my little guided excursion into the forest tomorrow. I'd almost forgotten about Professor Bonfils' offer to Lawson and for the reason of the trip in general until we got back to the conservatory.

We found Professor Bonfils sitting dejectedly at his lab desk, a sad frown etched into his features.

"What is it?" Lawson asked as we approached him.

Piers nodded to a tray in front of him, and we took a closer look. On it was the body of a dead Ulysses. Its bright blue wings folded, its inquisitive, curious light extinguished. "Our last breeding pair is gone."

Lawson's shoulders sagged, his whole frame seemed smaller. "Oh no."

I TOOK Lawson back to our hotel room. He was understandably quiet and sad. I put my keys on the table and cupped his face. "Tell me what you want. Do you want to talk? I know it helps you think straight talking through things."

He sighed and leaned into my palm.

"Lawson?" I said gently. "Tell me what's happening to the Ulysses."

He closed his eyes. "It's dying. The species. In captivity,

in the wild. Not just here, but worldwide. We don't know why."

"You think it's diet related?"

He nodded and looked up to me. "It has to be."

"Tell me why? Tell me how it's possible for just this species. No other butterflies are affected, so tell me what's different about this butterfly?"

He started to smile. "You really want to know?"

I nodded. "Start with the basics. You said this was happening worldwide. Where else is the Ulysses found?"

"Papua New Guinea, Indonesia, Solomon Islands."

"So basically, the tropics of the Pacific."

Lawson gave a nod and sighed. "Larvae feed typically on kerosene wood, citrus, and *Euodia*. Imago, they eat from blossoms of the doughwood plant."

"Okay, so what's happening to these plants to impact the butterfly?"

"By all reports, from various universities and the CSIRO, nothing. There has been some decline of the *Euodia* tree in deforestation, but that doesn't contribute to the fact they're dying in captivity."

"Okay, then, so tell me what's unusual about their deaths. It seems odd to me that they're making it to adult stage and then dying."

"Exactly. Typically parasites that may affect a butterfly species will render eggs unfertilised, or the egg casings are simply not viable."

"What is the main factors in adult Ulysses' deaths?"

"Heat stress, pesticides, predators such as snakes, frogs, birds."

"None of which can contribute to the butterflies at the conservatory."

Lawson shook his head slowly. "No. Everything is

organically grown and certified, from the national park, actually, and the conservatory is climate controlled. There are no predators."

"And it's only the Ulysses. No other butterfly?"

Now he sighed. "Just the Ulysses."

"It has to be botanical."

"That's what I said."

"Does Piers not agree?"

"He's tested the soil, the leaves. As have I. There are no significant changes; we've tested for every disease we can think of. Potassium was marked a little higher than usual but still well within the normal ranges. I've wasted three days re-testing when I should have been doing something else."

"Like what?" I asked. "What could you have done to avoid that butterfly dying today?"

He put his head down. "I don't know."

"Lawson, you had to start from the beginning. There's no point in studying a contaminated control sample."

"Maybe I should be here," he mumbled. "Full-time, trying to save this species."

My heart stopped.

His frown deepened. "The Tillman Copper is thriving; the Ulysses is not. My time would be better spent here."

"Oh." I nodded slowly. "You're right. It would be."

He put his forehead on my chest. "Though I can't bear to think of leaving you."

I rubbed his back. "We'll work something out," I said, not feeling the conviction I'd hoped he heard. "If it comes to that."

He looked up at me, his eyes imploring. "If I did decide to move here, would you support my decision?"

"Of course I would. I'd hate that you were so far away,

but we could make it work. I told you before, distance isn't a problem for me."

He settled his head against my chest and slid his arms around me. "Thank you."

I gave him a squeeze. "You're welcome."

"I'm hungry."

I snorted and lifted his chin so I could kiss him. "Then I shall feed you."

He let his forehead fall to my shoulder, and I kissed the side of his head. "Room service?"

He burrowed into my neck and hummed. "I wasn't talking about food."

CHAPTER SEVEN

LAWSON

I DON'T KNOW what it was about having Jack's arms around me, but it brought something out in me that I hadn't experienced with anyone else. Every time he embraced me, I felt safe and sheltered, in every sense of the word.

He also spurred a yearning, a deep physical desire within me. I wanted him to have me, claim me and own me. I wanted to be his, to fulfil every need he had, and to be thoroughly at his mercy.

His sweet, sweet mercy.

"Come with me," I murmured against his lips. "I want to show you something." I took his hand and led him to the bedroom. I urged him to sit on the bed, and I went to the drawer I'd put my underclothes in. "Now, please don't be mad."

I took out the two white envelopes I'd brought with us from home. The envelopes from the pathology lab concerning our bloodwork.

Jack's eyes went wide when he realised what they were. "Oh. You brought them with you?"

I nodded slowly. "I don't know why I wasn't ready before, but I am now." I swallowed hard. "If you are."

He still sat on the bed, his eyes were filled with worry. "I'm sure. Are you sure you're sure?"

I gave him a smile and sat down next to him. "Never been surer." I held up the two envelopes. "Do you want to read mine or yours?"

"Mine."

I handed him the envelope addressed to him and slid my finger underneath the seal of mine. I pulled out the folded piece of paper and opened it. Jack did the same, and we read our reports at the same time. My blood work was all fine, and I watched Jack as he read through his. He looked up and smiled, then handed me his report. I gave him mine, and after seeing his report was all fine as well, we sat in silence for a moment.

"What now?" he asked.

I took the letter from him, stood up, and set them both on the bedside table. Then planting my knee on the bed, I swung my leg over him to straddle his hips. "Jack, can I tell you something?"

He had to look up at me, his hands bracing his weight behind him. "Of course."

"I don't know if I will explain this adequately," I started, sliding my hand along his jaw. "I want to be yours."

He smiled in confusion. "You already are."

"No, I want to be only yours. I want you to make me yours, make me belong to you. In a way that no one else ever has."

His nostrils flared, his eyes flashed with desire.

I bent down and kissed him, tasting his mouth before I pulled away. I put both hands to his face and spoke against his lips. "Jack, I want to take you inside me, all of you, and only you. I want you to come in—"

Jack crushed his mouth to mine and flipped me over so I was on my back and he was between my legs. He drove his tongue against mine and kissed me so hard my brain lost all coherent thought.

I could feel his erection, hot and hard, against mine through our clothes, and then he was frantic about removing them. He sat back on his haunches and pulled at my shoes, giving me a chance to catch my breath. Then he undid my trousers and pulled the hems at my ankles to slide them off my legs. Then my underwear, then my shirt, until I was naked before him.

He took in every inch of my body and licked his lips. "Oh, Lawson."

Not that I minded being on display for him, being studied and ogled, not when he looked at me like he wanted to devour me. But one thing wasn't right. "You're still very dressed."

He pulled off his shirt, tossing it over his shoulder. Then he climbed off the bed and took his boots off, and while he undressed, I leaned over to the bedside table and collected the bottle of lube.

No condom.

My blood warmed at the thought of what we were about to do.

I flipped the lid on the bottle and Jack's head turned at the sound. "Put that down. That's my job," he said. His gruff voice sent a shiver through me. I snapped the lid shut and took a hold of my erection, giving myself a long, slow pull. He crawled onto the bed, up my legs, and stopped when his mouth met the tip of my cock. He locked gazes with me, let his tongue out, and licked the tip as I jerked myself off.

Then he slid his lips over my cockhead as I pumped the base, and he sucked me hard. I rolled my hips, urging him to take more of me, but he pulled away.

"Goddammit, Jack. Don't stop."

He smirked at me and continued crawling up until his mouth met mine in a hard, deep kiss. My cock forgotten, I gripped his hair and spread my legs, lifting my hips to meet his. He wrapped his hand around my knee and hitched my leg higher and ground his erection against me.

"Jack," I growled. I was fast running out of patience.

He pulled back so he was resting on his haunches. His thick cock jutted forward, almost right where I wanted him. He took the lube, slicked his fingers, and rubbed them over my perineum.

"Mmm," I hummed, raising my hips for him. "More, Jack."

He slipped a finger inside me, and I relaxed into it, knowing what I really wanted wasn't far away. Then he added another finger, sliding in and out of me, and I pushed down on him, needing more. "I need you inside me," I groaned out.

Jack leaned over me, still fucking me with his fingers. "I am inside you."

"Your cock, Jack. I need you to fuck me."

He grinned. He found something about my cursing during sex amusing. "There it is." He kissed me as he withdrew his fingers. "I know you've had enough games when you start to swear."

I considered cursing, and I considered demanding that he drive into me, but all I could do was beg. "Please, Jack. Please."

He poured lube onto his cock and slicked himself properly and wasted no time in positioning himself at my hole. He leaned over me once more, his eyes above mine. "Are you sure?"

I cupped his face. "Yes."

And so he pushed into me. Thick and breaching, hot and hard, and everything I needed. It was pain and pleasure, too much and nowhere near enough. Jack's eyes were closed, and his jaw clenched tight as he pushed all the way inside.

"Look at me," I whispered.

His eyes shot open and he groaned. "Lawson, you feel so good like this."

I brought his lips to mine. "So do you."

He moaned out a cry when he was all the way inside me, and he shuddered. "Lawson, I don't know how long... I can't last like this..."

"Then don't." I ran my hands over his face, taking in the depth of his restraint in his eyes. "Do what you want, fuck me if you need."

He pulled back and slammed into me. "Do you want to be mine?" he asked.

I nodded. "Please."

"Only mine?"

All I could do was nod.

He was annexing me in the most incredible way. Driving into me, filling me, and taking what was his. He hooked his arms underneath my shoulders, buried his face in my neck, and fucked me. Such a brutal tenderness; my cock rubbed between our bellies as he slammed into me but he held me like I was made of glass. Every fibre in my body, every strand of pleasure, every part of me belonged to him.

He bit my earlobe, then sucked on my neck, scraping his

teeth against my skin. "Prove it to me," he rasped, and it set off a reaction I couldn't stop. My body responded, a chord struck within me.

My orgasm buckled me, pleasure detonated like a bomb, and I came. My cock spilled between us, my whole body strung tight. I gripped onto his shoulders and arched my back as the waves of pleasure almost became too much to bear.

"Oh fuck, Lawson." Jack's voice was tight and strained. I opened my eyes to see him watching me, his gaze wide and filled with wonder. "I'm gonna come inside you."

I put my hands to his face and watched as his orgasm crashed over him. His eyes rolled back, his jaw strained and neck corded as his cock swelled and he came so far inside me.

In that moment, we were one. Physically, emotionally. I could feel his heartbeat pulsing inside me, through his chest, and it beat in time with my own. Resonating, completing, everything.

I'd never felt anything like it.

Jack shuddered as his orgasm subsided. I ran my hands through his hair and pulled his face back from my neck so I could kiss him. Deep and consuming, he thrust one final time and groaned in my mouth. His arms tightened around me and I knew without any doubt, he felt the same.

He slowly pulled out of me and rolled us onto our sides, pulling me close and wrapping me up in his safe embrace. "I love you, Lawson," he whispered in my ear. Then he cupped my face and looked into my eyes. "I love you, Lawson Gale."

I nodded, and my emotions crumbled. Like my heart was exposed to him and he cradled it with such tender hands, like a gift. I blinked back tears and all I could do was nod.

He froze. "Are you okay?"

Then I laughed through my tears. "So much better than okay."

Jack finally breathed and tucked me into his side, squeezing me. "Oh, you scared me."

"I'm just a bit overwhelmed," I admitted.

"That was very intense." He ran his hand over my back in reassuring patterns for a few moments, giving me time to breathe. Then he said, "We should get cleaned up. If you like, I could run you a bath, then I can order you some room service for dinner."

He was so protective, so nurturing. I felt completely adored and secure, and I had to admit, I loved letting him take care of me. I sighed contentedly and looked up to his perfect face. "I love you too."

He chuckled and put his huge hand on my face. "You're..."

"I'm what?"

"You look like you've been thoroughly had."

I smiled. "I have been. Every inch of me, thoroughly and completely, in the very best of ways. I'm not sure my skeletal system is back to solid form yet, so the bath may have to wait."

He kissed me with smiling lips. "Then let me get a cloth. You stay right here."

He peeled himself away from me and slipped out of the bed. I stretched out, feeling the most delicious aches in all the right places. Jack came back a moment later with a warm, wet flannel and took his sweet time wiping me down, following each caress of the cloth by a soft kiss and a hum of appreciation.

When he was done, he kissed the top of my shoulder. "Feeling like that bath now?"

"Mmm."

"Lawson, can I ask you something?"

"Of course."

"Do you have any regrets? About what we just did... no condom?"

"No regrets at all. Why? Do you?"

He barked out a laugh. "Uh, no."

"And you feel okay? Not sore?"

"I feel incredible. Do I not look like I feel incredible? Because I've never felt this sated. I'm not actually that well versed in physics, but I do believe you changed my bones from a solid to a liquid."

He chuckled, somewhat smugly.

I waited for him to look into my eyes. "Why do you ask?"

His smirk was salacious, and his eyes flashed with a heated look I was becoming quite familiar with. "Because I want to do it again."

I ARRIVED at the conservatory to find Piers studying a microscope, speaking to one of the lab assistants without looking up. They gave me a smile as they walked past. "Good morning."

"Quite," I answered, making Piers look up.

"Ah, Lawson. Good morning. How was your evening?"

The mere mention of last night brought with it a slew of memories and visual flashes of just how my night went. Sweaty bodies, quiet whispers, grunts and moans that felt so real a shiver rippled through me. Followed by a blush. I pretended to be distracted and focused on the microscope. "Very good. What are you studying in the slides?"

"The scales of the Ulysses that died yesterday."

"Find anything?"

He shook his head.

It was then I noticed the dead Ulysses on a tray behind him. It was fully intact. "Is that...?

Piers nodded. "The final remaining Ulysses was found dead this morning."

I sighed. Maybe Piers was right. Maybe my time was better spent here. The Tillman Copper was thriving and would do so whether I was there or not. The Ulysses, however, needed all the help it could get.

Moving here, away from Jack, was not what my heart wanted. But I couldn't, in good conscience, turn my back on a threatened species.

"Where is Jack today?" Piers asked, rescuing my mood somewhat.

"I just dropped him off at the park. He's spending the day doing what Parks and Wildlife officers do."

"He's a good man," Piers added. "I'm sorry if my being forthright with you earlier was unwelcome. I didn't mean to question your loyalty to him."

"He is a good man," I stated, probably with more finality than was necessary. But I was done discussing personal matters with Piers. That's not what I was here for. "So I've been thinking about the Ulysses. Are you familiar with entomotoxicology?"

Piers frowned. "The analysis of toxins ingested by arthropods that have fed on carrion?"

"Yes. Primarily it is testing on maggots and beetles that have fed on human remains to test for toxins in the body at the time of death."

"How is that relevant here?"

"Bioaccumulation." The blank stare he gave me told me he wasn't familiar with this. So I explained, "Bioaccumulation occurs when an organism absorbs a toxic substance at a faster rate than that at which the substance can be lost by catabolism and or excretion."

"I know what bioaccumulation is. What are you suggesting, Lawson? They're being poisoned?"

"My suggestion..." Then I corrected myself. "My professional opinion is that we surrender the Ulysses specimen to the CSIRO for entomotoxicological analysis, *specifically* toxicology reports."

His face resembled a cartoon character's. He went a furious red like a rising thermometer, and I half expected steam to come out his ears. "Surrender it?"

I stood my ground. "Yes. They have the proper testing facilities."

"They'll destroy it. To run such tests, they'll need to destroy it."

"They'll have to, yes."

He shook his head. "No. We can learn more from it as it is. I can pluck a few scales from the underside of the wing to analyse under a microscope, but to suggest they pulverise it..." He finished by shaking his head again.

"Professor—"

"No. These are the last species in captivity anywhere in this country. And you're suggesting we allow them to put it in a blender?"

Well, that was a crass way to put it. "Yes." I looked at the dead Ulysses in the tray. "You'll learn nothing from it as it is."

"We can run tests here. And we have! Dozens of tests."

"That found nothing."

"I thought you said it was their diet? What, now you've changed your mind?"

"No. Something they're eating is killing them. And entomotoxicological analysis would determine that. It's not like I'm asking to take a living specimen and euthanise it. It's already dead."

Piers stared at me for a long moment. "Arguing will get us nowhere."

"Then don't argue with me."

"What if you're wrong?"

"I'm not."

He waved his hand in the air to signify he'd had enough of this conversation. "Then get me proof. If you can prove something is affecting the diet of a species found in several different countries, poisoning them, then I will agree to the CSIRO testing."

SO, for the rest of the day, I sat in the lab, researching, studying, thinking. I scoured the internet for any information pertaining to toxins that might possibly attribute to the cause and effect I was suggesting. I read research papers on bioaccumulation, biotransformation, bioconcentration, biodilution. By four o'clock, I was well past hungry, and my vision was blurry. I paused only a moment to rub my eyes when my phone buzzed in my pocket. It was Jack.

"Hello," I answered, sounding tired, even to my own ears.

He, on the other hand, sounded excited. "Lawson, I think I found something you might wanna come take a look at."

"Jack, I'm very busy. I'm sorry. The last Ulysses died,

and Piers has said the only way he'll allow the testing I want done is to find proof."

"That's what I'm saying, Lawson. That's what I think I found! I think I know what's killing your butterfly. You gotta come over here. Bring Piers, he can have a look too. See whatcha both reckon."

The enthusiasm in his voice made my heart race. I had no clue what he could possibly have found in relation to a dying species of butterfly, but Jack was very clued in when it came to all things flora and fauna. He was excited about something, and that was enough for me.

I stood up and grabbed my keys. "Piers? Piers!"

The professor came out of his office. "What is it?"

"We need to go. You wanted proof. Jack thinks he might have found it."

CHAPTER EIGHT

JACK

I WAITED in the car park for Lawson to arrive, and I was practically buzzing. He pulled up right by me, and I started explaining before he was even rightly out of the car. "I spent the day with Gary, the guy you met yesterday. Well, this morning we went into the forested area where the public doesn't get to go, and he was telling me about how for the last few years the wet season hasn't been... well, wet. Well below average rainfall. And he was telling me about cane toads and how they're rampant with the drier weather."

By this, Piers was out of the car, and I'd gone to the boot of the rental and took out the plastic tub with Lawson's water testing gear in it. I handed it to Lawson and continued, "He said the water pools are smaller, more concentrated, and the cane toad tadpoles are even toxic. The waterways are making some critters sick. We need a good wet season and she'll be right then."

"Jack, where are we going?" Lawson asked.

I took the tub of specimen jars and closed the boot. "I'm getting to that." I nodded to the staff-only gate to the side of the main entrance and started walking in that direction.

"Anyway, then this afternoon, we went back to the orchard."

"The orchard we visited yesterday?" Lawson asked.

"Yep. Anyway, Gary and Elsie—she works here too—were telling me about the water reticulation system, how it drip-feeds the trees. We had a look at the tank and that's when I saw them."

I stopped at the gate, waiting for Gary to open it. "Saw what?" Lawson asked.

"Cane toads."

The door swung open revealing Gary and Elsie, the two park staff members I'd spent the day with. I quickly made introductions and we walked over to the old ute the staff used to drive around the park.

"Cane toads?" Piers asked. "What's the significance? They're everywhere."

"Correct," I agreed, putting the tubs into the back of the ute. Putting my hands on the tray back, I jumped up, then extended my hand out to Lawson first, helping him up, then Piers.

"Where are we going?" Lawson asked again.

"The orchard," I answered.

Gary jumped in behind the wheel and drove us slowly down to our destination. I looked at Piers, who didn't look all that comfortable riding in the back of a utility. It was kinda bumpy and windy, but there wasn't enough room for us all to fit in the front. Piers was holding on to the side like he might die any minute. I figured distracting him might help. "Piers, where does the conservatory get its fruit from? That it feeds the butterflies?"

"Uh, here. And another organic orchard on the other side of town."

Lawson, not bothered at all with riding in the back,

cocked his head to the side in that thoughtful-processing way he did. "Are you saying there's a correlation to the decline of the Ulysses and the cane toad?"

I nodded and grinned. "More specifically, the tadpole of the cane toad." They both stared at me, so I elaborated. "I know it sounds crazy, but think about it. Where are the Ulysses butterflies found? Tropical Queensland, Solomon Islands, Papua New Guinea, and parts of Indonesia. Where are cane toads found? Queensland, Solomon Islands, Papua New Guinea, and parts of Indonesia. The Ulysses butterfly lays its eggs on the *Melicope elleryana* tree, yes?"

Lawson nodded. "The doughwood tree, yes."

"And where does the doughwood tree like to grow?"

Lawson was beginning to smile. "Near water."

"And what lives in the water pools at the roots of the doughwood tree?"

"Cane toad tadpoles," Lawson answered.

I smiled at him. "And what did Gary say was highly concentrated and toxic?"

Lawson was beginning to smile. Piers looked sceptical. "How does this affect the Ulysses?"

"Bioconcentration," Lawson answered, grinning now.

I beamed at Piers but pointed at Lawson. "That big word he said."

We arrived at the orchard and Gary slowed the ute to a stop. I jumped out and stacked the tubs atop one another while they climbed down. "The water tank is over this way."

As we walked over to the storage tank for the reticulation system, Lawson further explained. "Bioconcentration is a term that was created for use in the field of aquatic toxicology. And if the cane toad tadpoles are increasing the toxicity of the water, as Jack suggests, it stands to reason that only the Ulysses is affected because only the Ulysses inhabits the doughwood."

We stood, looking at the tank, Gary included. The tank was pretty big: six-metre circumference, one metre high, and open at the top. We could see down to the bottom. It was essentially a rainwater catchment tank. The park administration buildings' roof runoff was gravity fed to the tank. The water was then drip-fed to the orchard trees.

Lawson turned to Gary. "Are we free to take water samples?"

"By all means," he answered.

So, Gary and I stood there and watched as they took water samples in specimen jars and even managed to catch some tadpoles.

"Cane toads are generally land-dwellers but they lay eggs in water," Gary said for everyone's benefit. "They're a real bloody pest. We cover this tank, but it doesn't stop 'em. They were introduced to Australia to eradicate some kind of beetle, but they ate everything else except for the damn beetle. They've infested waterways all across the top end of the country. Almost killed off water monitors and quokkas over on the west coast and have no predators. A mate of mine lost his dog to toad poisoning."

"How do you deal with them here?" I asked.

"We try to trap 'em and euthanise 'em. We're organic here, we have to be."

"Yeah, back in Tassie we have the European white snail. Different pest, and certainly not on this scale, but same principle."

Lawson and Piers were finished with their water samples, so we moved to the trees themselves. Ulysses favoured citrus, so we went to those first. Lawson collected bark, leaf, and fruit samples. He collected another water sample of the drip feed irrigation near the trees, and of course, documented it all accordingly.

I thought Piers might have been reluctant to agree with my theory; he seemed a bit standoffish. But then he asked Gary, "And the fruit collected for the conservatory comes from here?"

Gary nodded. "Yes."

Piers frowned. "And the doughwood trees in our butterfly house?"

"Sourced from the forest. We sell the saplings to raise money. There was a push a while back for the public to plant doughwoods when the decline of the Ulysses was first announced." Gary spoke in a no-nonsense manner. He knew his job. I liked him.

Lawson stood up from his collection of specimen jars. "Can you take us into the forest?"

Gary looked at his watch. It was getting late. "We'll have to be quick."

So we grabbed the tubs and climbed into the back of the ute. Lawson smirked at me when Piers opted for the passenger seat, and once we were seated in the tray back and Gary was driving us further into the forest, Lawson leaned in and gave me a quick kiss.

"I believe I've said this before, but you're a godsend."

"Maybe it'll lead to nothing," I said modestly.

Lawson shrugged. "Maybe. But I've spent the whole day studying and researching all kinds of biotransference, biocontamination, biotoxicity... but something was missing. I couldn't piece it together. Then you mentioned this, and it fits, Jack." He gave me a smile that made my ribs feel too tight. "At any rate, if it's not the toxicity from the tadpoles, it's something like it. At least this should allow Piers to agree for me to send samples to the CSIRO for testing."

"What do we do if it *is* the tadpoles?" I asked. "They've been trying to find ways to get rid of the cane toad for decades without any luck."

Lawson seemed to think it over a while. "I don't know."

He seemed saddened by the idea, and my first instinct was to rescue him. "Hey," I said, putting my hand on his leg. "But if it is, then at least we'll know. Then contingency plans can be put into place. We can act, and there'll be a better chance at saving them, right?"

He stared at me until his smile won out. "You know what I love most about what you just said—and for the record, I loved all of it—but the way you say *we*. *We'll* know, *we* can act. I love that you're including yourself in this, not only because it's important to me, I understand that, but also because it's important to the conservation of a species."

I nudged his elbow with mine. "True. But mostly because of you."

He gave me one of his shy smiles, my favourite kind. But before he could speak, the ute slowed to a stop and Gary got out. "This is as far as I can drive. We're on foot from here."

Lawson quickly jumped out. "How far is it, and what gear should I bring?"

"You won't need your sat phone or anything like that," I elaborated, knowing what Lawson meant. "This is where we came this morning. It's only a hundred metres or so but it's not exactly easy going. We'll just grab some more samples, then we'll have to leave. It's getting late."

Piers looked at his watch, while Lawson, Gary, and I all looked at the sky. It was funny how different we were. I mean, I understood why Piers might have fancied Lawson, truly I did. He found his intelligence attractive, and his love for *Lepidoptera*. But Lawson was so, so much more than that.

Lawson slid his backpack on regardless, then picked up the one tub that had the empty specimen jars in it. "Right then. Which direction?"

"East," I said with a smile because I knew Lawson would get it. He turned due east and started walking, while I'm sure Piers was more of a left or right kind of guy.

I had to wonder how long it had been since Piers had set foot in the field. Or if he had, ever. It wasn't that I didn't like the guy. I just didn't like the fact he kept blocking Lawson from trying to move forward with his help on the Ulysses. Why ask him here if he was just going to say no to every suggestion? I mean, if Lawson did decide to stay on here and help, he and Piers would argue every day. Lawson certainly wouldn't back down. I didn't think he knew how to take a backwards step.

Then again, maybe Lawson liked to be challenged. Maybe he liked the heated professional discussions and debates. Maybe he liked someone who challenged him on an intellectual level...

Lawson stopped walking. "Jack?"

"Yeah?"

"Is this the spot you saw this morning?"

There was a bit of an embankment that housed shallow pools of surface water lined with doughwood trees. I'm pretty sure Lawson knew it was where I'd meant to bring him. I nodded.

"You okay?" he asked quietly.

"Sure," I said, faking a smile.

He eyed me cautiously for a moment, but Piers and Gary were right behind us. Soon enough, Lawson and Piers were taking water samples, tadpoles, a leech or two, bark and leaf samples, soil samples, and discussing things like equilibrium partitioning models and other things I couldn't pronounce, let alone follow.

"Guys," Gary interrupted their discussion on particulate toxin ratios. "We need to get going back. Park'll be closed soon, and without permits, you have no insurance to be here."

Lawson conceded and packed everything into the tub. I held my hands out. "Want me to carry it?"

He graced me with a smile. "Thank you." He handed it to me, then opened the backpack. He pulled out a bottle of water and handed it to Piers, who I hadn't realised was kinda sweaty. Then Lawson quickly took out a notepad and pen, some digital thermometer thing, and proceeded to jot down some notes.

"What are you writing?" Piers asked after taking a mouthful of water.

Lawson didn't even look up. "Temperature, humidity, location. Standard stuff."

I couldn't help but feel a bit proud of him. Gary gave me a smile before he turned to head off back the way we'd come. Piers followed Gary and I waited for Lawson.

"You good?" I asked after he slipped the notepad back into his backpack.

He slung the backpack on and settled the bag on his back, then we started the hike back to the ute. "Never better. Though I would like to come back, trek further into the forest if we can."

"Sure. Though we'd better organise the proper permits."

Gary dropped us back at the information centre where the rental car was parked. I picked up the three tubs stacked on top of the other and loaded them into the backseat. "I'll sort out those permits before they close," Lawson called out, dashing into the administration office.

I went to follow him, but Piers stopped me. "May I have a word?"

"Sure."

He looked around, embarrassed. "I take it Lawson told you I had expressed an interest in him joining my team here."

I nodded slowly. "Yes, he did."

"He hasn't exactly answered."

"Are you telling me this because you want me to try to sway his decision in your favour?"

"No, no," he said quickly, then I'm sure he mumbled something in French under his breath.

"Because if you did, then you really don't know Lawson at all."

He nodded slowly. "He is a feisty one."

"He's also very good at his job, and he's rarely ever wrong. Maybe you should listen to him."

He seemed offended. "I hope you know I mean no ill toward yourself and Lawson."

"I know. I also know that you expressed interest in his joining more than your team."

Piers put his hand up. "I admit it was true. But he told me, in no uncertain terms, his only interest in that regard lies with you. I told him you were a lucky man."

Okay, I officially didn't get this guy. Was he confronting me about my relationship with Lawson? Or was he congratulating me? "Piers, what is it you want from him?"

"I want him to help save the Ulysses."

"Then listen to him. You know, before when I said Lawson's rarely wrong, that was true. But you know what else he is? Level-headed, and his eyes are always on the end result. If he *is* wrong, he simply takes the new information on board, learns from it, and moves forward. He has no ego when it comes to his job. You can call him the best and brightest and he'll agree with you, but that's not ego. That's a fact. He doesn't care for fame and glory. I mean, he found a new species and named it after someone else. That right there tells you the kind of man he is."

Piers nodded. "I know."

"So if he does decide to stay here to help you with the conservation of the Ulysses, it's because he thinks it's the right thing to do. Not because of anything you or I say."

Lawson came out of the office holding some papers. He held them up victoriously. "Permits for tomorrow granted!"

He handed them to me and I read the first part. There were only two names on the form. Me and Lawson... and it was an overnight stay permit.

"Overnight?"

Lawson blinked. "Well, the cane toad is primarily nocturnal, is it not?"

"Well, yes."

"And I assumed Professor Bonfils would not rather camp out overnight?"

Piers glanced at me, then smiled at Lawson. "You would be correct."

Lawson tilted his head in an of-course-I-am way then grinned at me. "It also means I can spend all day analysing our samples with Piers and sending away for further test results, while you organise our camping gear."

I grinned at him. "Sounds like a plan." Sounded better than just a plan. A night in the tropical rainforest with just Lawson and me sounded perfect.

Lawson pulled out the car keys. "Right, then. Let's get these samples back to the lab."

CHAPTER NINE

LAWSON

I GOT to the lab early, excited to start my day. Professor Bonfils was there already, as I assumed he would be.

"Good morning." He looked behind me. "Where's Jack?"

"He dropped me off. He needed the hire car to get some camping gear for tonight," I explained. "I hope you weren't offended by my not including you. I assumed you'd prefer not to camp out, sleeping on the ground."

He chuckled good-naturedly. "You assume correctly. No offence taken. My days of field work, as such, and nights on hard earth are well behind me." He seemed thoughtful for a moment. "I think Jack might prefer my absence also."

I withheld a sigh and bit my tongue. Jack had told me of the conversation they'd had while I was sorting out camping permits. While I did think Piers had accepted that I'd rejected his advances, Jack wasn't sure. In fact, he wasn't sure what Piers' intentions were at all. I'd reassured him the professor was simply eccentric and probably most accustomed to luring any younger man he wanted with his French accent and confidence. Jack had laughed.

"Possibly. Though Piers, please understand his concerns are of my wellbeing, not a reflection of any insecurities you think he might have. He asked if I was comfortable working with you, and I said yes. If I wasn't certain of your professionalism, I wouldn't be here."

Piers fought a smile. "You are one of a kind, Lawson Gale."

"Thank you. Now let's get these samples processed."

SO THAT'S what we did. For hours, we sat side by side documenting, citing, researching, collating. It was therapeutic and productive. Piers called his associate at the Cairns CSIRO, a lady by the name of Jamine. They'd collaborated before, so when he asked if she could process some findings on behalf of the conservatory in the interest and conservation of the Ulysses butterfly, she not only agreed but said she'd fast-track the reports.

By the time Jack arrived, a little after three in the afternoon, we were ready to ship our samples and preliminary findings off to the CSIRO for further, more comprehensive testing.

"How'd it go?" Jack asked. "Can you determine anything yet?"

"The soil samples have the higher potassium levels that the soil we tested here has," Piers said. "It could be a direct correlation to the introduction of the toxins into the water."

"That's good, right?" Jack asked. "I mean, not good that the soil is affected, but good for the theory that it's all linked."

"Yes." I gave him a smile. "Did you get everything we might need tonight?"

"Yep. It's gonna rain later, apparently, so the girl at the camping store threw in an extra canopy tarp for free."

I almost laughed. I could just imagine Jack talking shop with the sales assistant, making her laugh and charming her enough to give him something for free. He probably even offered a sightseeing tour of his national parks if she ever finds herself in Tasmania. "I'm sure she did."

Jack beamed, then looked at all the individual bagged, sealed, and labelled samples, slides, and the paperwork that went with them. "Is this everything you have to take over?"

I nodded. "Yes. Fingers crossed we get some kind of feedback. Any kind, at this point, is all we can ask for."

Piers put two insulated boxes on the counter, and we carefully stacked our samples into them. Before I sealed the second box, Piers came back holding a square, clear plastic container. Inside it was one of the Ulysses that had died. I knew he was reluctant to surrender the specimen for research, but in his heart he knew it was for the right cause. We needed to see if there were any traces of the toxins in the butterfly. It was the only way to know for sure if we were on the right track.

I took the container. "Thank you, Piers."

"It is for the best," he replied. "I will keep the other one, but if they require it, then I'll... then I'll surrender it also."

I put my hand on his upper arm. "You're doing the right thing."

Jack carefully lifted one of the insulated carry boxes. "We good to go?"

I picked up the second box. "Yes. They're expecting us."

Thankfully the drive to the CSIRO laboratories didn't take too long. We were greeted by Jamine in the front office, and Piers made introductions. She was younger than I assumed, appeared Polynesian, though I never asked, and wore a white lab coat. She was friendly enough, and excited by the prospect of finding anything to help in the conservation of the Ulysses. I liked her immediately. Piers and I followed her into the restricted area, while Jack offered to stay in the waiting room.

"Okay," she started, looking at her clipboard. "We will start with the water samples, testing for bioaccumulation factors, and see what readings we get. Then we'll move onto the plant samples, checking for degrees of transference, then finally the animal samples. You said you collected tadpoles, leeches. And there's a butterfly sample?"

"Yes," Piers answered. "The last butterfly to die at the conservatory."

"We're hoping there's a correlation between the deaths of the Ulysses and toxins from the tadpoles," I stated. "Looking for bufadienolides specifically, the toxin from the tadpoles."

Jamine looked from her clipboard to me. "You think there's transference to the food source via toxins from tadpoles permeating the water?"

My answer was resounding. "Yes."

She looked at Piers. "And you?"

He took a breath and seemed to think about his answer. "I will admit, I didn't at first. But I do now. I think it's plausible, yes."

"I'm going back out tonight," I admitted. "I'm hoping to collect more water and doughwood samples from different locations. If the Ulysses is dying in the wild, then we need broader samples."

Jamine nodded. "For conclusive results, yes."

I had no issue with that. "So, we start here. If it's positive locally, then we take it further. Regionally. Nationally. Internationally."

"Well," Jamine said, going back to her clipboard. "It wouldn't be the craziest thing we've found." Then she looked at us both and gave us a blinding smile. "Leave it with me."

When we left the lab, we found Jack in the waiting room. He threw the magazine he was reading back on the table and stood up. "How'd it go?"

"Good, hopefully. Jamine's going to fast track it," I answered. "Reading anything in particular?"

"Nah, just a guy I went to school with got a write-up. It's nothing." He brightened. "So, we ready to go camping? If we want to make good headway into the forest, we're gonna need to make a start or we'll run out of sunlight."

I grinned at him. He was clearly looking forward to a night in the great outdoors, as was I. Piers threw his hands up with a laugh. "Okay, okay, you two, enough with the love-eyes. But please drive me back to the lab first."

A SHORT WHILE LATER, we were hiking into the forest. Gary had graciously driven us as far as the ute would go, and Jack had packed everything expertly into the backpacks we now lugged through the dense undergrowth. We each carried a tub of specimen jars, clip-seal bags, and identification forms, and it was hard going. It was humid, and the uneven forest floor didn't exactly make for easy hiking.

Jack used his GPS and compass and led the way, and I followed. He weaved the way down to a gully, which was dotted with water pools. He put his tub down and surveyed the puddles and trees. "Well, they're pretty dried up now, but I'd reckon this'd be almost a creek with decent rain."

I put my tub alongside his and took out the folded paper map from my backpack. I found where we were. "Yes, see here?" I pointed to the area on the map. "There's a blue line that runs east. But it's certainly not a creek now."

"Nope." Jack opened the first tub and took out some specimen jars. "But it's supposed to rain tonight, remember?"

"It rains most nights in the rainforests. Funnily enough, that's why they're called rainforests."

Jack let his hands fall to his sides and he stared at me. "Are you being sarcastic?"

"I was going for roguish."

He laughed. "I'm the roguish one, remember?" He shoved a specimen jar at my chest. "Now, go get your toxic water samples. I'll take samples of the roots and leaves."

He trudged off, and I quickly took my water samples and even captured another tadpole. I documented the jars, cataloguing each sample, and we went further on, deeper into the national park, and took more samples before the setting sun got the better of us. "We should set up camp," Jack suggested, looking around the small clearing at the top of the dry creek bank. "You wanna do the fire or the tent?"

"Fire."

Jack rolled his eyes and dumped his backpack. "Thought you'd say that."

I had a campfire roaring by the time Jack declared the tent was ready. I collected the small skillet and found the food Jack had packed. Vegetable pasta salad, which I understood perfectly. The clip-seal bag of flour, however, had me confused. "Uh, Jack?" I held up the bag. "I take it this is actually flour and we're not suddenly drug mules."

He laughed and climbed out of the tent. "Yes, it's flour."

"What for?"

"You'll see. I'm making dessert. Is the pasta salad still cold?"

I felt the outside of the container. "Yes. Um, what dessert can you make in the middle of the forest with a resealable bag of flour?"

Jack rifled through the insulated food bag and pulled out what he needed. A tin of Carnation Milk, some portions of butter I suspect he borrowed from the hotel, and a bottle of water. "And the pièce de résistance," he declared, holding up a small bottle. "Golden syrup."

He added the butter to the bag of flour first and re-zipped the seal. He rubbed it in the bag, then added the wet ingredients until he effectively had a dough. He added it to the skillet, wrapped it in foil, and shoved it into the coals of the fire. "And while it bakes, we eat the pasta. I wasn't too keen to have meat in the insulated bag," he mumbled as he rummaged for the forks. He held one out to me victoriously, and I took it with a smile. "So pasta salad with Mediterranean vegetables it is."

"And a true Aussie bush damper for dessert," I added.

He smiled as he took a mouthful of pasta. He looked particularly handsome with the fading sunlight and flickering firelight; a sight I would never tire of. "So," he said as we ate, "thought any more on the possibility of staying on here in Queensland?"

I chewed and swallowed slowly, giving myself a moment to get my thoughts clear and my words even more so. "Truthfully, I haven't yet decided. My heart says no..."

"But your conscience is telling you yes."

I sighed. "This species is dying. The Tillman Copper is doing okay, and the breeding program is well established.

Once the vegetation has regenerated in the woodlands near Scottsdale, they can be released. I'll need to monitor that, of course, but for now..."

"I get it, Lawson," Jack said quietly.

"It's only an idea I'm considering. I can't really make a decision until we get results back from the CSIRO." I frowned. "I don't want to leave you. Please tell me you understand that."

He met my gaze and offered me a knowing smile. "Of course I do. I get it, Lawson. I really do. And like I said before, I have no problem with long-distance relationships. If we need to travel to see each other, with you up here and me back in Tassie, then that's what we do. Simple as that."

"That's why I love you," I murmured. "Well, that, and your damper-making skills."

"Oh!" he cried, reaching for the skillet. He carefully pulled it out of the fire and, with a towel, lifted back the foil. He poured in the golden syrup and recovered it. "Two more minutes."

We finished the pasta salad, then Jack dished up two steaming plates of what he called 'cocky's joy,' an old-fashioned Australian bush dessert. Simple and utterly delicious.

"Oh wow," I said around a mouthful of syrup-sweetened damper. "This is amazing."

Jack laughed as he ate. "I knew you'd like it." We ate the rest in silence, and Jack was looking around the darkening campsite. "So, how long till we see cane toads?"

"Soon."

He nodded slowly. "So... Do we have enough time for a lesson in biotransference?"

I wasn't sure what he meant. "A lesson? What do you want to know? I thought I explained; it's the result of biological substances being absorbed by another living organism."

Again, he nodded slowly, though this time he smirked. There was a smouldering darkness in his eyes that I knew well. "Oh, I know what it is all right, but I thought I could give you a practical lesson, perhaps."

"Oh." Heat pooled in my belly. "*That* kind of lesson."

Twenty minutes later we had dinner cleaned up and squared away and we were stretched out on the thin mattress in the tent. Fully dressed, making out, kissing, touching, gripping, and grinding.

I broke the kiss and offered him my neck, which he quickly adored with kisses and teeth. "I thought you wanted to do this outside?"

"It's gonna rain," he murmured against my skin.

He was right. The humidity was high and thick with the need to break for rain. Or maybe it was just how hot it suddenly was in the tent.

"I've been thinking about this transference thing," he continued, finding his way to the hollow between my collarbones. He settled himself on top of me properly, grinding his erection against mine. I tried to unbutton my shirt, but his hands were quick to stop me, and he pinned my arms at my sides. His lips were swollen, his eyes burned with desire. He spoke against my mouth. "And how it applies to when we make love."

I understood his meaning. Now we made love without condoms, every time he came inside me, it was a transference. God, I could barely speak. "I think I need a reminder."

His salacious grin was my reward. I thought my blood might catch fire.

Jack let go of my arms and knelt astride me, then reached for a backpack, I assumed for lube. I seized the opportunity to unbutton my trousers and roll over onto my stomach. I lifted my hips and pulled my pants down just enough to expose my arse to him.

"Lawson, what are you doing?"

I put my forehead to the mattress and slid my arms above my head. "I want you to have me, Jack. Just like this. Right now, as I am."

He paused a moment. "I don't want to hurt you."

"Do you have lube?"

"Yes."

"Then just do it. Now, Jack. I really need this."

"Let me stretch you first."

Even the thought of anything else inside me right this minute besides what I wanted most drove me crazy. And not in a good way. "Jack, please just fuck me. I don't want fingers, I want your cock. Inside me. Now."

The sound of his zipper in the silence sent a warm thrill through my bones. I heard the pop of the lube bottle lid, a delicious wet noise, and he slicked himself. I arched my back, raising my arse. I didn't need to see what he was doing. I could hear it, and it somehow made the anticipation even better, hotter. The slide of cool liquid down my crack didn't quell the fire in me. It seemed to fan the flames.

With his left hand planted beside my head as he leaned over me, he slid his hot, hard cock along the cleft of my arse.

I was all out of patience for games. "Jack."

Then his blunt cockhead was pushing inside me, and it was far too much and still not enough. He whispered in my ear. "That what you wanted?"

It was a keening sound that escaped me, and he froze.

"Yes," I managed with a groan. He was so big and breaching, yet I relished the burn, the intrusion. The feel of him inside me was everything. "Give it to me."

Jack let his full weight press on my back, his mouth at

my ear, his hands gripped my hips, and he started to rock back and forth. "Mmmm," he moaned as he thrust slowly in and out of me, deeper with each pass. He took his time with me, eventually pushing harder and faster. "I won't last long. You feel too good."

"Then this might be a lesson in bioaccumulation," I said breathily. Jack's bubble of laughter became a groan, and he quickened his pace. "See how many times you can come in me."

My words brought him undone, and he slid one arm underneath my chest and held me as he came. I could feel everything... he was everything.

Jack slumped on top of me, his body wracked with the aftershocks of his orgasm, and eventually his breathing returned to normal. His words were warm against the back of my neck. "I never want to move," he mumbled.

"Then don't."

He nuzzled the hair at my nape. "You didn't come."

He normally made it his mission to bring me to orgasm first, and it was strangely satisfying that this time he hadn't. As though my sole purpose was for his pleasure. "Next time."

He hummed a nonsensical reply, but after a moment, he rolled off me, but keeping his arm wrapped tight around my chest, he manoeuvred me so I was his little spoon. He slipped out of me, just as the first spatters of rain began to fall on the tarp above the tent.

I felt bereft at his absence inside me, and as though he felt the same, he snuggled into me. He was sleepy, sated. "So, about that bioaccumulation..."

CHAPTER TEN

JACK

SWEET MOTHER OF GOD, he felt good. And that filthy mouth of his was my undoing, again. I wanted to stay inside him forever. I wanted to keep him in my arms forever. The rain got heavier and the sound of it, the warmth of Lawson against me, was lulling me to sleep. The rainforest sang a different song in the rain. Fewer birds, more frogs, drumming out a tempo that was oddly soothing.

Through the tent I could see the campfire become dimmer as the rain doused its flames and little by little our only light was gone. I closed my eyes and I remember thinking *I'll just snooze for a moment. I'll just close my eyes for a second before we go out looking for cane toads in the rain.*

I WOKE UP WITH A FRIGHT. It was dark, and something was wrong. I was alone. Lawson. Where the hell was Lawson? Then I noticed how heavy the rain had gotten outside, thumping down on the canopy tarp above the roof of the tent, and I had no clue what the time was. I fumbled in the darkness for a lamp and switched it on. Lawson was most definitely gone. So were his boots, the second lamp, and one of the tubs.

Shit, shit, shit. I didn't mean to fall asleep.

"Lawson?!" I called out.

I checked my watch. 11:47 p.m.

"Lawson?!" I yelled, pulling on my boots and a poncho raincoat. I pulled the hood over my head and went out into the torrential rain. "Lawson?"

"Yes, I'm over here," a voice called out.

I turned to the sound and could see him then. Well, I could see the light of the lamp through the dense trees. Pure relief washed over me like the rain. "What the hell are you doing?" I yelled out and walked toward him.

He grinned, wearing a rain poncho, but was still soaked to the bone. "Taking samples. Toads love the rain."

Jesus Christ. I called out, "Please tell me you're wearing gloves."

He held up his free hand. "Of course I am."

I pulled on the hood of my poncho so it shielded more of my face. "It's pissing down." I slid in the undergrowth on my way towards him; a mix of mud and dead leaves made for slippery footing. Eventually I got to where he was and I didn't have to yell. "Why didn't you wake me?"

"You were sound asleep. I could hear the toads, so I thought I'd get up and take a look. I haven't been out of eyesight of the tent."

I knew he wasn't foolish. He was a competent hiker. "Well, I'm out here now. What are we doing?"

His smile became a grin. "I want to go further up this trough, follow the edge of the creek." He pointed north. "I didn't want to get too far from camp, but now you're up..."

"Want me to head south?" I asked. "We'd cover twice the ground."

"Sure." He opened the tub and gave me two specimen jars. "Don't go too far. The ground's slippery, so be careful."

I rolled my eyes. "Are you lecturing me on terrain safety?" He laughed, and I shook my head at him. "How can you be so happy? It's midnight, it's pouring rain, and we're standing in a rainforest surrounded by cane toads."

His answer was simple. "Because it's midnight, it's pouring rain, and we're standing in a rainforest surrounded by cane toads."

I couldn't help but laugh. "I think I deserve a midnight, rainforest, rainy kiss." I pointed to my mouth.

He happily obliged, planting his lips on mine. "Don't touch the cane toads."

"Yes, boss," I said, instead of rolling my eyes. Only an idiot would not know that cane toads were poisonous.

And with a final smirk from Lawson, we went our separate ways. The sooner we got this done, the sooner we'd be back in the dry tent working on that bioaccumulation theory...

I never knew science could be so much fun, and I certainly never knew it could feel so damn good.

I almost felt the need to track down my year eight science teacher and apologise. With a snort at my hilarious thought, I jumped down into the shallow gully to collect some more samples. The fresh water from the rain in the pools would dilute the toxins, we would assume, but samples must be taken to compare. This was the boring part of science. I much preferred the practical, private lessons on the transference of *biostuff*, and knowing Lawson was out there with *my* biostuff still inside him made my chest bloom with warmth that expanded to my groin.

God, I was never going to have enough of him now.

I sat the lamp down in the mud and collected a sample of the water. On closer inspection, or maybe it was because the water level had increased, I could see a string of toad eggs along the edge. Scooping up as many as I could, careful not to touch them, I screwed the lids on, pocketed them, and set about going back to find Lawson.

The small slope was slippery as hell. My boots sunk into the mud and I cursed the weather and all of Far North Queensland as I clambered up to the top. My pants were now pretty much wet right through, and I was cursing that too as I made my way back to where I'd left Lawson.

It wasn't long until I saw his lamp, and I headed straight for it. It was still raining—a torrential downpour, in fact. The forest protected us a bit, but it was still heavy. If we had this much rain in this amount of time back home, we'd be two feet underwater. I slipped in the mud but thankfully didn't fall, but then I cursed about that as well, mumbling to myself, "Who the fuck can live in this?"

"Oh, hey," Lawson said. He was crouching down, looking at something on the ground, but he smiled when he saw me.

"What are you looking at?" I called out, not five metres from him, but the rain was heavier, louder.

He laughed. "Two cane toads copulating."

Of course, that's what he's watching. "Is cane toad porn a thing?"

"I certainly hope not. It's disgusting."

"Don't get too close," I warned. Jesus, he was right near the deep edge of the gully that was fast becoming a creek. "Can you take a step this way?"

Lawson stood up, and as he did, the ground underneath

him gave way. The entire bank of the gully, Lawson, his lamp, and the cane toads were gone.

"LAWSON!"

I lunged after him, but it happened all too fast. One minute he was there, and the next he wasn't.

"Lawson!"

I got to the edge, careful of my own footing, and heard a groan. I hung my lamp over the edge and saw him. "I'm all right," he said weakly, spitting out dirt and muck, wiping his mouth with his sleeve.

He was on his back, about two metres down, covered in dirt and mud from where the bank had given way. His lamp was out or under the dirt or under water; I wasn't sure. It was dark down there.

"Can you move?" I asked, trying not to panic. "Stay there, I'll find a way to come down."

"No, it's okay," he said, starting to get up. "Ugh!" He picked up a clump of dirt from his chest and threw it. No, it wasn't a clump of dirt at all. It was a cane toad. Fuck.

"Lawson, are you okay?"

He got to his feet awkwardly, slipping in the mud and sloshing in the water. "Yes, yes. I'm fine."

I sat my lamp beside me and lay down on my stomach, reaching my arm down toward him. "Take my hand."

When he put his hand in mine, I'd never felt so relieved. With every ounce of strength I had in me, I lifted him to the top. He was covered in mud and gunk, but I didn't care. I threw my arms around him. "God, you scared me."

"Scared you?" he asked meekly.

I put my hands on his muddy face. "Are you okay?"

He nodded. "Just a little shaken. The ground just gave way."

Instinctively, I pulled him further away from the bank. "The rain must have weakened it. Come on, let's get you back to the tent."

He certainly didn't argue. I grabbed the lamp, took his hand, and led him back to camp. At the front of the tent, I pulled his rain poncho off over his head so most of the mud and gunk wouldn't come inside with us. His trousers and boots were caked, but there wasn't much I could do about that. I pulled him inside and sat him on the bed.

But before I could take his boots off, I noticed him lick his lips, then again, and he made a face like he tasted something bad. "Lawson? What is it?"

"Tastes like metal. Like mud and sludge but metallic."

Oh no.

I noticed the mud smeared down his face and neck was streaked with white. A milky-like spray over his mouth...

Oh no, no, no.

I grabbed a bottle of water and screwed the lid off. "Wash your mouth out. Don't swallow. Spit it outside."

He tipped the bottle to his mouth, swished, and leaned over through the door to spit it out. When he sat back upright, he swayed and closed one eye. "Oh, my Lord," he said feebly. He put his hand to his head. "Oh, my head." Then he put his hand to his chest, over his heart, and his breathing became laboured.

"Lawson, we need to get you to hospital. Now."

He didn't answer. He just slumped to the side and almost fell off the mattress. I caught him and tried to hold him up. "Lawson!" I shook him gently. He tried to open his eyes but couldn't. "Lawson?"

Nothing.

I let go of him so he slouched to his side on the bed, and I grabbed the backpack with the phones and keys in it. I fumbled for my phone and dialled ooo. "Ambulance, please." The dispatch lady was quick to respond, and I gave her all the information I could: cane toad poisoning by ingestion, unresponsive. But the thing was, we were in the middle of the rainforest, a good half-hour trek from the track Gary had dropped us off at. There was no way an ambulance was going to rush to the tourist car park, then wait for God knows how long until I could walk us out of here.

Thankfully the dispatcher had her wits about her. "I'll put a crew on standby, call us again when you're almost there.

"Will do."

I shoved the phone in my pocket, slung my backpack on, then dragged Lawson to a sitting position. He was floppy and kept falling to the side. I had no idea how I was going to carry him out of the jungle and hold a lamp in the pouring rain in the middle of the night and find my way to the track, let alone the car park. But I certainly couldn't give up. I heaved him over my shoulder and crawled out of the tent. I grabbed the lamp and stood up in the rain. He moaned over my shoulder. "Lawson, baby. I got you. We just need to go for a little walk."

I took a second to get my bearings and headed off in what I was sure, what I hoped, was the right direction.

The ground was slippery, I could hardly see, and I couldn't wipe the rain from my eyes. Lawson wasn't heavy, by any means, but he was dead weight over my shoulder, and I had to step over tree roots and up and down natural step formations on the path. It wasn't even really a path. Walking *into* the forest had been easy. It had been daylight, it had been dry, and I hadn't even considered the footing.

Walking out of the forest was a different story altogether.

After what felt like a lifetime, I stopped, sure I'd taken a wrong turn. Nothing looked familiar in this light, or lack thereof. I considered changing direction, but Lawson moaned. "Hang on," I said, not knowing if he could hear me. I worried about the blood rushing to his head and to his heart. I worried about what that would do to the toxins already in his body.

I had to move quicker.

Instinct told me to keep going. I really had no clue if I was going in the right direction, but something told me I was. And after an eternity, the forest cleared to a track, the very track that Gary had dropped us off at. *Oh, thank God.*

The ground was flatter, the tyre tracks making it easier to walk. There was a proper path to follow, at least. I picked up my pace, trying to shuffle Lawson a little to make him more comfortable. He groaned. "Almost there, baby. You're okay. Gonna get you some help."

I fished my phone out of my pocket. Not slowing down my pace, I dialled ooo again. After explaining who and where I was, I was assured an ambulance was on its way. The dispatcher asked me to stay on the line until the ambos arrived, and I had to admit, I was grateful for the company.

My legs burned, my back hurt, but my heart... my heart was in limbo. That unsure place between hope and breaking, being scared to death and never feeling more alive.

"He's gonna be okay, isn't he?" I asked into the phone.

The dispatch lady, whose name was Cheryl, gave me her professional, noncommittal answer. "You've done everything right. ETA for the ambulance is five minutes, they'll assess him and get him straight to hospital."

"No one's died from cane toad poisoning, have they?" I asked.

"Not in Australia, I believe. Dogs and cats, yes. Other native wildlife, yes. Humans, I'm not sure. The hospital has been notified."

"It sure is dark out here," I said, not even realising the rain had stopped until that very second. My breath was short and I choked back tears. "He has to be okay. I don't know what I'd do if he's not."

"Mr Brighton."

"Jack."

"Jack," Cheryl said calmly, "just keep on moving. Can you hear sirens? See any lights?"

I listened for a moment. "The forest is really loud." God, it was deafening. Crickets, cicadas, frogs, toads, birds... I thought most birds were mostly diurnal. Maybe it was the blood pumping in my head that made everything seem so damn loud. I pulled the phone away from my ear so I could concentrate, and...

In the distance, I could hear them.

"I can hear the sirens," I said into the phone, and pulling strength from a place I didn't know existed, I started to run. Lawson moaned again. But then I caught a glimpse of red-and-blue lights and headlights. "I can see lights!"

I heard Cheryl telling someone—not me, maybe the ambos—that I had a visual of lights, they should be seeing me any moment now.

I broke into the clearing that was the car park, just as the ambulance arrived. "I'm here," I said, to Cheryl, to God, to anyone.

The ambulance made its way over to me and stopped. I'd never been more grateful to see anyone. Then they were lowering Lawson onto the gurney and I was telling them what happened while they were strapping him on and checking his eyes, and I was bundled into the back of the ambulance with him, and then everything was quiet.

And I could finally breathe.

My body ached, my chest burned.

"You okay?" the paramedic asked me, looking up from Lawson.

I waved him off, stuck the heels of my hands into my eyes, and willed myself not to cry. Taking a few deep breaths, I gathered myself to finally get a good look at Lawson.

And I immediately wished I hadn't.

There was a line of foamy drool running down the side of his mouth, escaping under the oxygen mask. His shirt was ripped open, he had ECG pads stuck to his chest, but his face was pale. Too pale.

He looked... dead.

"Is he...?"

The paramedic wouldn't answer me. Instead he spoke into some kind of radio mouthpiece, giving readings and stats I couldn't follow. The driver replied, "ETA, one minute."

I slowly reached out and slid Lawson's hand into mine. "Is he going to be okay?"

The paramedic finally afforded me a sorry look. "His heart rate isn't good, but there's a cardio specialist—"

Lawson abruptly coughed and vomited, and the paramedic launched into action to ensure Lawson wouldn't choke. The ambulance came to a stop, the back doors flew open, and there was a flurry of noise and movement, nurses and doctors, bright lights and too much noise.

Then they raced Lawson inside and I was still standing there, alone, confused, scared. Numb. The world seemed to spin without me, and it was like I couldn't move.

A kind face appeared in front of me. A heavy-set man in scrubs with blond-and-pink hair, an eyebrow ring, and an empathetic smile put his hand on my arm. "Are you with him?"

I nodded.

"You were the one who brought him in?"

I nodded again.

He tried to gently pull me toward the emergency doors. "Come on, let's get those scratches looked at."

Scratches? I looked down at myself. I had scratches up my arm which I didn't recall getting, and there was blood soaked through my muddy trousers at the knee. I didn't recall that hurting either.

"My name's Lyle," the nurse-guy said. "You wanna come inside? We'll get you looked at, then we'll see what we can find out about your friend."

"His name is Lawson," I said. "He's my boyfriend. Well, he's more than that. He's the guy that changed my life. He's everything to me, and I can't go in there because what if he's not okay? What if I go in there and he's not doing so great? Because if I stay out here, then no one can tell me he... no one can say that he's not..." I swallowed hard and shook my head. "I don't think I can go in there."

Lyle rubbed my arm. "Oh, sweetie. He's in the very best hands." I looked at him then, into his eyes, and whatever he saw in mine made him frown. "What's your name, honey?"

"Jack."

"Well then, Jack. I need you to come with me." This time he pulled on my arm and I went with him.

Being led through the emergency department was like an alternative reality in slow motion, the fluorescent lights, the nurses and doctors all moving without sound. There was a disconnect somewhere in my brain.

I found myself sitting on a hospital bed in a sterile cubicle. I watched as Lyle swabbed the scratches, cleaned and dressed them. I still couldn't feel anything. Then Lyle was asking me questions about how I felt. Did I feel nauseous, have blurred vision, shortness of breath? Was I allergic to anything?

I shook my head. "Nothing. I need to see Lawson."

Lyle nodded but just continued with his assessment, writing down notes. He didn't understand. "I need to see Lawson."

He began to shake his head.

"Is it because I'm not family? Is it because we're gay? Would it make any difference if we were married because—"

Lyle put his hand on my knee. "Hon, you can't see him right now because the doctors are working on him. They need space and calm to do their jobs. If you go in there, you'll disrupt the space and calm, and they won't be able to do their jobs. Being gay don't change anything, not for me. You listen to me, sweetie. I promise you I will keep you posted. You will know all there is to know. I will find out all I can, okay?"

He looked at me with such sincerity, I could only believe him. I nodded.

"Good," he said with a smile of satisfaction. Then his eyes focused above my right eye. "Now, let me take a look at this cut up here."

Until then, I hadn't been aware of any cut above my eye and instinctively tried to touch it, but he held my hand. "Nuh-uh, no touching. Not until we've cleaned those hands."

Then I noticed that my hands were covered in dirt and mud, and there were scrapes across the knuckles.

Oh.

"So, you banged yourself up pretty good," Lyle noted, wiping a cotton swab above my eyebrow."

"I didn't realise," I mumbled.

Lyle nodded like that was expected. "You've been through a bit tonight, huh? Did you really carry him all the way out of the national park? In the dark?"

I nodded. *Of course, I did.*

He gave me a sad smile. "That'd explain the state you're in. Want some Panadol?"

I shook my head. I couldn't feel anything.

Other nurses came in, then a doctor. They all fussed and talked stats, but I didn't pay any attention. I couldn't focus at all. I stood up off the bed and Lyle and the doctor put their hands on me to stop me. "You need to stay here," the doctor said.

"I need to find Lawson."

Lyle frowned. "I'll go and see what I can find out. You stay here so I know where to find you. I'll be real quick."

He disappeared through the curtain. The doctor shone his penlight in my eyes and asked me all the questions Lyle already asked, and I sat there for I don't know how long. Forever, it felt like. Then Lyle came back and put his hand on my knee. "Okay, so he's stable."

I let out a breath, instant tears welled in my eyes. "Oh, thank God. Can I see him?"

Lyle shook his head. "He's not in the clear yet, Jack. The toxins cause all sorts of stress on internal organs, primarily the heart, so they're monitoring him pretty closely. He's still unconscious. They're running all types of blood tests and watching his brain activity. They've got him in the ICU. I can take you to the waiting room because you'll only be sitting up here waiting, so you may as well sit there and wait. You'll be closer, but you won't be able to see him until the morning, at least."

I nodded, feeling the first flicker of hope. "Thank you."

Lyle filled in some more paperwork, and I was soon following him through a warren of corridors and elevators until the sign on the wall read Intensive Care Unit. Lyle pulled some chairs without armrests into a line. "That's the closest you'll get to a bed. At least it's padded," he said. He disappeared for just a second and came back with a folded blanket. "Get some sleep. It's three o'clock in the morning."

I nodded, but apparently that wasn't enough. Lyle made me sit down then lie down the best I could. He put the blanket over me, asked if I was okay one last time, gave me a gentle pat on the shoulder, and was gone.

I closed my eyes, just a blink, because I wanted to stay awake in case Lawson woke up. But the next thing I knew, there were voices and a gentle hand shaking my arm. I opened my eyes to a strange woman's face. I had no clue where I was, who she was, or why my body ached from head-to-foot.

"Sorry to wake you. Lyle said you'd want to be there when Lawson woke up."

"Lawson," I mumbled, then tried to get up. My body protested, every muscle, every bone, but I pushed through it with a grimace as I got to my feet.

"This way," the nurse said. "It's still early, but I can take you in for just a sec."

I followed her with my heart in my throat, and she stopped at a door at the end of the long room near the nurses' station. I peered in, and there he was. Lying in the bed, propped up into a half-reclined position. There was a doctor at his side, but I couldn't take my eyes off him.

He was still pale, his eyes half-open, he had oxygen tubes up his nose, and he looked like he'd been to hell and back. Then he saw me and cracked half a smile, which set me in motion. I was through the door and at the side of his bed—opposite his doctor—in four long strides, and without really thinking, I wrapped my arms around him and pulled him against me. Literally, almost pulled him completely off the bed. "Oh, my God, Lawson, I've never been so scared," I mumbled into his neck.

"Okay, sir," the doctor said, pulling on my arm. "You need to let him go."

Lawson squeaked, and I quickly propped him back up in bed. "I'm sorry. I'm sorry," I said, patting him down, trying to make sure I hadn't hurt him. "I just... I just..." Then the tears started. Relief and every emotion I couldn't name right then flooded through me and burned hot in my eyes. I put my forehead to his.

Lawson put his hand to my cheek. "Jack."

I pulled back and wiped my eyes, then kissed the side of his head. The doctor cleared his throat, making me look at him. "Sorry," I mumbled, not really sorry at all.

"You're the one who saved his life," the doctor stated.

Lawson closed his eyes and smiled. "He has a habit of doing that."

"He has a habit of almost dying," I said with an incredulous laugh. "Anyway, I didn't save him. I just got him here so you could do the saving part."

The doctor smiled at that. "He's very lucky."

"Is he going to be okay?" I asked, taking Lawson's hand. He had a cannula taped to the back of it, so I had to be careful.

"Right now, he needs rest. We'll run more tests later, but being conscious and alert is promising." The doctor looked at his watch. "I suggest you get some sleep."

With that, he was gone. I leaned down, took Lawson's face gently in my hands, and kissed him. "I love you. Go to sleep. I'm not going anywhere."

His eyes remained closed, but the corner of his lip lifted in a smile.

I pulled a chair over to the side of the bed, sat down, and carefully took his hand. I tried to stay awake just to watch him, but my eyelids betrayed me.

The next thing I knew it was daytime.

CHAPTER ELEVEN

LAWSON

I FELT AWFUL. Worse than awful. Like I'd been hit by a bus. A fleet of buses. Like each bus had backed up and mowed me down again, in fact. I couldn't actually pinpoint which part of me hurt the most. Every part of me ached and stung. My bones felt like razors, my lungs burned with every inhale, my head ached like a white-hot poker was embedded in my brain. Even my skin hurt.

I blinked until my eyes would stay open, and then I saw him.

Jack.

He was in a chair beside the bed, sound asleep, leaning forward with his head near my hand. It took every modicum of strength to lift my arm and touch his hair with my fingers. He stirred, then shot up. "Lawson," he croaked. "Oh, thank God you're awake. How're you feeling? You scared the crap outta me." His eyes welled with tears. "Jesus, you scared me."

He had a gauze bandage above his eye. "You okay?" Wow, it even hurt to talk.

Jack laughed and squeezed my hand. "I'm fine. So much better now you're awake."

Then I realised he had scrapes on his knuckles. "You've cut your hand And above your eye."

Jack shrugged it off. It seemed he couldn't take his eyes from my face. He leaned in and pressed his lips to my forehead, then he cupped his hand to my cheek. "How are you feeling?"

"Awful."

He frowned. "I'll go get the doctor. Be right back."

I closed my eyes again for just a moment, and when I opened them again, Jack was standing beside a tall woman in a white coat. "Mr Gale," she said with a smile. "Nice to have you with us." She leaned in and shone the light of hell into each eye.

I clamped my eyes shut in response. "If you're checking retinal dilation, would you mind not piercing my brain?"

I heard Jack's snort of laughter. "Oh yeah. He's okay."

"No, I'm not," I disputed, still with my eyes closed. "Everything hurts." I suddenly felt nauseous. "Ugh."

The doctor told of side effects, speaking of pain, severe headaches, nausea, just to start with. "I'll be back soon. Lawson needs to rest, but we'll need to do liver and kidney function tests."

"Can he have anything for the pain?" Jack's voice was like a homing beacon. "He said everything hurts. There has to be something you can give him."

Their voices muffled, and I drifted into sleep. But the feeling of queasiness never waned, and I woke up with a start, needing to vomit. Jack, who was now sitting beside the bed again, lurched forward with a sick bag. I dry heaved into it, producing nothing but bile, reminding me that my entire body had been through a mince grinder.

I fell back against the bed, and Jack soon had a damp cloth to my forehead, wiping down my face. I closed my eyes but lifted my hand for him. He knew what I meant because he threaded our fingers, and I fell back asleep.

The next time I woke, it was because there were people talking close by. A familiar voice, and I blinked again and again to try and focus. I realised belatedly that my drowsiness must be chemically induced. But Jack was still sitting beside my bed, talking into his phone.

"Oh wait, he's just waking up." He held the phone to his chest and smiled at me. "Hey. How're you feeling?"

"Better."

"They gave you something for the pain and nausea."

I smiled. Well, I think I did.

Jack held up the phone. "It's your mum."

"Oh."

"Want to speak to her for a second?"

I nodded. "Sure."

"Okay, Hyacinth, I'll just put him on. He's drowsy and he can barely keep his eyes open, but here he is."

Jack put the phone to my ear and held it there. "Oh, Lawson," my mother cried into the phone. "We've been so worried."

"'S okay, Mum." I smiled again at Jack. "Jack's looking after me."

"He carried you out of the rainforest on his back. In the dark and in the rain. I don't know what we'd do if not for him. You would have died out there."

It took a minute for her words to connect in my brain. "Yeah. He's kind of wonderful." The words felt like molasses in my mouth.

Jack took the phone back, and I was going to tell him to put it back to my ear but I couldn't stay awake.

"Yes, Mrs Gale. He's nodding off again. I will. Of course. Yes, I'll call you later. Okay, bye."

Then warm lips pressed again to my forehead. "That one's from your mum." Then he softly kissed my lips. "And that one's from me."

<hr>

THE NEXT TIME I woke up, Jack was thumbing something into his phone. "Hey."

His gaze shot up and he sat forward in his chair. His phone forgotten, he took my hand. "Hey. You look a bit better."

"Drugs are good."

He laughed quietly and put the back of my hand to his face. For a moment he closed his eyes and when he looked at me again, he sighed. "Oh, Lawson."

He looked exhausted, and the white strip of bandage above his eye had some spots of red on it. His knuckles were scraped and there was another gauze strip on his arm. "You okay?"

He nodded slowly. "I'm perfectly fine. Worried about you, mostly."

"Sorry."

He gave me a sad smile. "Do you remember what happened?"

I thought back. My memories were a little hazy. Whether that was drug-induced or because of the toxin, I didn't know. "The bank of the gully collapsed."

Jack nodded. "And you and two cane toads went with it. From what I can tell, they somehow fell on or near your face and secreted toxins into your mouth. Doctors said it must have been a direct ingestion for you to be so ill. I told them you wiped your mouth as you got up, and there was milky stuff in the mud smeared all down your chin and neck."

"I remember... the taste was... metallic and... putrid."

"If you're tired, close your eyes," he murmured. "I'm not going anywhere."

I shook my head a little. "What have they given me?"

He afforded me a smile. "They had to do some tests first, to see what your kidneys and all that could handle. But something for pain and vomiting. I can't remember what they called it."

I squeezed his hand, feeling my strength drain away. "What time is it?"

"Five-thirty in the afternoon. I'm probably supposed to be leaving soon but I think they took pity on me." He bit his lip and even blushed a little. "I might have told them we were engaged to be married so I could stay with you. Hope you don't mind."

Even half-sedated, his words sent a thrill through me. A machine next to me beeped erratically. "I don't mind," I said.

Jack looked at the machine, and the smile he gave me was knowing. And smug. "Mmm, this ECG machine right here tells me you rather liked the idea."

A nurse appeared and walked straight over to the machine, reading something. "Ah, you're awake, Mr Gale. Is Jack here making you excited, or is there some other reason your heart rate spiked?"

I didn't need to answer. The heat across my cheeks said enough. Jack laughed, and the nurse patted him on the shoulder. "Be gentle with our patient, please, Jack." She made some notes in a file, then on a computer, and smiled to herself as she walked out.

Jack lifted my hand so he could kiss my knuckles.

"ECG machines don't lie."

"Shut up."

He laughed louder this time, then stood up and kissed my lips. Of course, the ECG beeped again, but I could only smile.

"Ah, he's awake," a familiar voice said. I looked to the door to find Piers holding a bouquet of flowers.

Jack sat back down, but never let go of my hand. "Yes, he's more alert this time."

"This time?" I asked. My brain was so foggy.

"Piers came in this morning," Jack explained, "when he heard the news."

Piers walked into the room and put the flowers beside my bed. "Yes, Gary came by asking if I'd seen you. He went to your camp today and found it deserted and everything left askew like you'd abandoned it in a hurry. He was concerned when he saw the embankment had washed away."

"So Piers called your phone," Jack explained further, "which I had here in the backpack. I told him what happened, how sick you were. And he came by to check on you."

"And brought Jack lunch," Piers declared loudly. He waved his arm with that dramatic flair he used so well. "This boy has not left your side. He refuses to leave, so I had to feed him or he'd starve."

Jack smiled at Piers, and it was clear whatever animosity had been between them was now gone.

Piers gently patted my shin. "You look better, Lawson. Before you looked like death, but now you have some colour."

"I feel a little better. Hazy, a little slow, but I'd rather that than the headache I woke up with." Jack rubbed my hand, which felt really nice and reminded me that my skin didn't hurt anymore either.

"The doc said you'll probably have headaches for a while," Jack said. "And you'll be weak and tire easily."

I smiled. "Feels about right."

"Well, I'm glad you're feeling better," Piers added.

Then I thought of something he'd said a minute ago. God, my mind really was slow... "Our campsite? The samples we took, the data..."

Piers smiled. "Gary collected everything, camping gear, samples, and whatnot, and brought it in. I have all your work catalogued and waiting for you. I didn't want to touch it without your permission."

I tried to wave him off but my hand—the one Jack wasn't holding—felt like lead. "Please, do what you will with it. I'd rather we not waste any more time."

Piers gave a hard nod. "I'll start on it first thing. But now, Lawson, you need to rest. I can see you're in very capable hands. I'll be back tomorrow."

He waved us off, and Jack smiled at where Piers had stood. "You and he are more amiable?" I asked.

"He means well," Jack said. "He was worried about you, but he said he's very glad you have me." He shrugged. "Kinda can't argue with that."

I smiled and took in a deep, steady breath. I wasn't sure which parts of me were starting to hurt again. Under the chemical buffer of drugs they'd given me, there was a current of pain just waiting.

Jack seemed to understand. He picked up the pain-relief push button. "Want me to press this?"

I shook my head. "I don't want to sleep again just yet."

"Tell me what you want?" He took my hand. "If it's within my power..."

"Food."

Jack snorted quietly before a grin spread across his face. He stood up and softly kissed my forehead. "Let me go see what I can find out."

Twenty minutes later, he was spoon feeding me a broth soup. Clear liquids apparently, and under normal circumstances, I'd have probably objected—and Jack turned his nose up at it—but it was the best tasting soup I'd ever had.

I could only stomach half of it, getting incredibly full all of a sudden. I left the jelly and cup of tea for later, but I was suddenly exhausted and achy all over. Jack asked if I wanted him to push the pain-relief button. I gave a nod and closed my eyes. I felt his lips on my forehead before sleep claimed me.

———

I WOKE up feeling so much better and to a freshly showered, smiling Jack. "Good morning!" Again with a kiss to my forehead.

"Morning," I said, my voice croaked.

"How are you feeling?" He asked, with a hopeful look on his face.

"Better." I sat up, feeling every protesting muscle. "And I'm starving."

"That's a good sign." Jack propped up my pillow and pressed the automatic lever on the bed so I was more comfortable sitting up. "I think I heard the breakfast trolley. Surely you can have some proper food today."

"I hope so."

"If they say no, I'll sneak you in some."

"No you won't," a nurse said as he walked in. He had a stripe of pink hair and metal rings pierced into his face in random places.

"Ah, Lyle," Jack said happily. He stood up and shook hands with him. "Good to see you again."

"Just came in to see how the patient is," Lyle said, looking to me. Then he spun on his heel and looked at Jack. "Well, patients." He inspected Jack's face and hand and arm. "You healed up quite nicely. And you, darling"—he turned back to me—"had this man just about beside himself." He did something with the machines and checked my saline bag, then leaned in and winked at me. "You know, in case he didn't tell you, he said he'd marry you if that's what it took for us to let him stay with you."

I felt the colour return to my face, and Jack cleared his throat and gave me an apologetic look. "Uh, yes," I replied. "He told me something of the sort."

"Just as well," Lyle said with a cheery grin. "'Cause there's a line-up of girls and guys who'd be happy to take him up on his offer."

Now Jack blushed. I gave Lyle my best attempt at stern. "Thank you, but I should think he's spoken for."

Lyle just laughed. "You can have yourself a light break-fast, my good man."

"Oh, thank goodness, because I'm starving."

I was sure the toast was stale, and maybe the toast was cold, but it was all good. And I was certain the hot tea was brewed in heaven. Jack watched me devour everything with an amused, enamoured look on his face.

It was only once I'd eaten that I'd taken a moment to think about the morning. "You left last night?" I asked him.

"Yeah, I needed to shower. To put it bluntly, not even

my charm and good looks could mask the fact that I stunk." He offered me a small smile. "And you were sound asleep. I was back first thing."

"Have you eaten?" I asked. "I should have asked before I mowed through my breakfast."

Jack snorted. "Yeah, grabbed a coffee and toastie from Maccas on my way."

"You said you'd marry me. And you told them we were engaged? Did I remember that?" My memory of yesterday was all but a blur.

Jack held my gaze, even though I was certain he'd rather looked around the room or anywhere else than at me. He swallowed hard. "I did tell them that, otherwise they might not have let me stay. And I would. Marry you." He lifted his chin, as if defiant and proud and nervous. "I would."

The ECG machine started to beep like crazy, and Jack laughed as Lyle came in to investigate. "I need to have these removed," I said, pulling at the circle pad stuck to my chest. "They're giving all my secrets away."

Lyle laughed. "I'll speak to the doctor."

"Lyle? I'd like to have the catheter removed and the saline as well. If I'm allowed. And I'd really like to go home today."

"No promises," he said, walking out in search of my doctor.

"Do you feel up to it?" Jack asked when we were alone.

"I'm sick of being hooked up to everything. I'm certain the doctor will wish to see if I can keep food and water down before they agree to discharge me, but I feel okay. I'm tired, and I'm sure I could manage pain medication on my own. And I'd really like to shower. And shave. And brush my teeth. I feel disgusting."

Jack put his hand to my face and swept his thumb across my cheek. "You're still exhausted, though. I can see it in your eyes. Don't rush yourself, my love."

It was as if him mentioning being tired put me under a spell because a wave of weariness washed over me. Maybe it was the big breakfast I'd eaten. Maybe it was all the talking, but I blinked slowly. "I am tired."

He pressed his palm into my cheek and traced my eyebrow with his other hand. "Then sleep."

So I did.

I WAS RIGHT about the doctors wishing to see if I could eat and drink, and by mid-afternoon, I was fast out of patience. I was, however, unhooked from all machines and urine bags and allowed to shower.

Lyle offered to help, but Jack was quickly on his feet. "Need me to help instead?" Then he must have realised how keen he sounded because he followed it up with, "I mean, I can look after him. Here, and when we leave eventually, I'll be the one who's helping him, so should I learn here first?"

Lyle fought a grin but gave him a side-eye. "All right. But no funny business, you hear?"

Jack gave him a Scout salute.

"And you press the assistance button on the wall in the bathroom if you need help, okay?"

Jack collected the shaving bag, made sure I had towels waiting for me in the ensuite bathroom, then helped me stand up. He held my arms and watched my feet. "Just take it easy. If you need to rest or stop, tell me."

"I'm okay." We shuffled to the bathroom, and Jack started the water while I caught a glimpse of myself in the mirror. I was taken aback by how pallid I looked, accentuated by the bruise-like smears under each eye. "Good Lord, I look awful."

"You've been through a bit, don't forget," Jack added. "And anyway, you look perfect to me."

I turned to look him in the face. "No funny business, remember?"

He chuckled quietly. "Believe me, that's the last thing on my mind right now."

I undid the hospital robe and let it fall to the floor. "The very last thing?"

"Yes." He took my arm and supported me as I walked under the water spray. "How about we just worry about you getting well first, huh?"

The water felt heavenly. Divine, even. I washed my hair, scrubbing the grit of dried mud from my scalp, cleaned my body and face the best I could, and let the hot water run over me. I must have swayed a little because Jack was soon holding my arm. "Okay, that's long enough," he ordered.

Then I was sitting in a bathroom chair and he was drying me down with a towel, gently, lovingly. I didn't have the energy to argue with him about drying myself, but it was also a very tender moment between us.

Then Jack knelt before me with my pyjama bottoms in hand. He fed one leg in, then the other, then pulled me to my feet so he could pull the pants all the way up. It just so happened that my groin was right near his face. He looked up at me and licked his lips. "Okay, so it's not the very last thing on my mind." He stood up quickly and let out a deep breath. "I'm only human, okay?"

I chuckled quietly, secretly pleased I still had an effect

on him. "Not sure I have the strength for it right now anyway."

He pulled a T-shirt on over my head, and I fed my arms through the armholes. Then he scooted my chair over closer to the basin. "Can you brush your teeth from there?"

I nodded, so he drew a strip of toothpaste onto my toothbrush and handed it to me. Brushing your teeth after a few days of not being able to was a little piece of minty-fresh paradise. I almost felt human, apart from feeling exhausted and achy, but I was led to believe that was to be expected.

When I was done with my teeth, I scrubbed my hand over my scruffy jaw. "I don't think I could be bothered shaving." The truth was, I was already exhausted again.

Jack chuckled. "I like the three-day-old growth on you. I say leave it."

I motioned for him to come closer with a curl of my finger, and when he was close enough to kiss, I nuzzled my cheek to his. "You like that?"

He made a strangled groan sound, and took a step back. I took that response as a yes. "Back to bed with you," he said. "And no teasing."

Jack helped me get settled, and I was almost dozing off again when the doctor came back in. "Good news," he announced. "You can go home. All your results have come back clear. On the proviso that if the headaches get worse, any dizziness, nausea, you get yourself right back in here."

"Of course," Jack answered, nodding.

"I'll get the discharge paperwork ready. No kissing any more cane toads, ya hear?" the doctor joked.

I snorted. "I'll keep that in mind."

He walked out and literally had to sidestep Piers as he was walking in. "Oh, look at you! So much better."

I gave him a smile. "I feel better."

"Did I hear you're allowed to leave?" he asked.

"Yes. Thank the heavens."

"That is good news." Piers grinned. "And I have even better news..."

I suddenly wasn't so tired. "What's that?"

"Jamine contacted me, little over an hour ago. The CSIRO has results on the samples we took over."

"And?"

"And they're going to do a lot more testing, Lawson, because you were right. The Ulysses is dying of bufadieno-lides poisoning, directly related to the biotransference from the tadpole of the cane toad to the doughwood tree, on which the Ulysses larvae and pupa feed. Levels are low, but enough to affect the caterpillar, so the butterfly weakens soon after the time it reaches imago."

I sagged against the mattress, relief coursing through me. "Oh, that is fantastic news."

"Yes! But it is just the beginning!" Piers said. His excitement would have been contagious if I weren't so damn tired. "There is much to be done. Now we know the cause, we need to implement strategies and plans. But having the CSIRO on board is hugely beneficial—"

I was sure he could have talked for hours. "Piers, I'm not staying."

The smile left his face and the air left his lungs in a resigned sigh. "I assumed as much, Lawson. After you were so ill and Jack took such good care of you, I figured you'd go back to Tasmania."

"There's still a lot of work to be done on the Tillman Copper," I added, feeling the need to justify my decision. I glanced at Jack. "And it's where my home is."

Jack grinned, and Piers nodded. "I get it. Love is a beautiful thing, blah blah blah."

I chuckled. "Something like that." A quiet fell over the room for just a moment. "Piers, I would officially like to offer my services, though. If you need to discuss or even think-tank with someone, I insist you call me. I'd still like to be involved, to help, although from a distance. Not here."

Piers gave a grateful nod. "I will hold you to that."

"I can recommend some names of people who may be able to assist you."

"Indeed. But for now, you should rest."

Jack shook his hand. "We'll drop around to collect our camping gear tomorrow or the morning after. I'm sure Lawson will want to see the lab one more time before we leave."

"Then I shall leave our farewells until then," Piers added with a flourish, a wave of his hand, and he left.

Jack walked slowly back to my side and traced a line over the back of my hand with his finger. "You don't want to stay here? In Queensland? I'm sure there's a lot of work you could do…"

I took his hand and threaded our fingers. "No. I want to go home. Back to Tasmania. Where I belong, with you and Rosemary."

Jack looked so happy he could burst. "I'd like that too."

I kissed his knuckles, then leaned back on the inclined bed and sighed. "I really miss Rosemary. Have you spoken to Remmy?"

"Of course. Rosemary's just fine. Luca's tilling his vegetable garden, so Rosemary has been helping every day." Jack brushed my hair off my forehead. "Remmy was very worried about you."

I smiled up at him, feeling the weight of exhaustion settle over me. "I miss her as well. I know she and Nico are your friends, but they've come to be dear to me too." I think

I was mumbling, so tired, I just had to close my eyes for a minute.

Jack kissed my temple. "They love you too."

CHAPTER TWELVE

JACK

LEAVING the hospital with Lawson was the best feeling ever. He was exhausted, and he still looked pale. He was to manage the headaches and body aches with Panadol and Advil, which he was loath to take, but he did—which told me he wasn't as well as he pretended to be.

When we got back to the hotel, I propped him up on the sofa with pillows and a blanket, and he dozed for a bit. I watched him while he slept and contemplated just how much he'd changed my life.

Six months ago, I was intrigued, bewitched even, by this butterfly man. Now I was in love with him, impossibly so. Impossible because there was no going back from this. I was a changed man. My heart belonged wholly to him, and I knew, without a doubt, it always would.

God, I thought I'd lost him this time for sure. And it really put things into perspective for me.

When he'd gone back to save the Tillman Copper in the path of the raging bushfire, I thought I might lose him then too. But looking back, I could see now that was adrenaline.

This time it was fear.

God honest, heart-stopping fear.

I thought he was dead. I thought I'd lost him forever, and I'd never been so terrified in all my life.

And to see him now, sleeping all peaceful and safe on the couch in front of me, made me truly understand that I couldn't live without him.

And that scared me too.

In a good way. In a life-affirming kind of way. In a my-life-is-forever-changed kind of way.

I resisted the urge to touch him, even just to stroke his hair or his beautiful cheekbone, in fear of waking him up. So I tidied up our clothes, did some washing, getting everything ready for our flight home the day after tomorrow.

Lawson was keen to go tomorrow if we could change flights, but the doctor suggested another full day of rest would be best, so that was that.

I ordered some room service for our dinner, knowing he'd probably wake up starving again, and went into the bathroom to freshen up. When I came back out, Lawson was sitting up on the sofa, bleary-eyed but smiling.

"Did I wake you?" I asked him. "I was trying to be quiet on the phone to reception."

He shook his head. "It's fine. You ordered dinner?"

"Yep. I put in a special request for plain vegetable and chicken pasta. It might be a little bland, but I thought the protein and carbs might do you good."

"Sounds perfect." He slowly got to his feet and walked gingerly over to me. "Thank you for looking after me. For saving my life, for being you."

I brushed my lips against his. "You're most welcome."

He looked at me all dreamy with a loving smile, then added, "I really need to pee."

I laughed. "Need me to help you with that?"

He gave me a sly smile as he shuffled to the bathroom. "I think I can manage."

After dinner, which he devoured, we curled up on the couch together, me being the big spoon, to watch some TV. He yawned, then sighed heavily, and was already struggling to keep his eyes open. "Sorry," he murmured. "I know this isn't how we planned to spend our holiday."

I gave him a gentle squeeze. "I'm just glad you're okay."

He wiggled his butt against my groin. "Yes, but still... I'm sure I'm not that sick that I can't enjoy some—"

I put my hand on his hip to still him. "Ah, that's not helping. And you heard what the doctor said."

Lawson grumbled. "Well, yes. Complete rest for the next few days."

"And I'm sure that means no strenuous activity. And believe me, the way we have sex is quite the workout."

He chuckled. "But I could just lie there, face down, and you could—"

"Lawson, that's really not helping." Jesus, the visual of that, the feel of him against me, and my dick was well and truly awake.

"You really won't have sex with me?"

"Not until you're feeling better."

"I'm fine," he protested but followed with another yawn.

I kissed the back of his head and wrangled my way from behind him to get off the couch first. Then I took his hand, "Come on, bedtime."

And even if he really desperately wanted to have sex right now, there was just no way. He could barely lift his head as it was, let alone keep his eyes open. I got him into bed, slid in beside him, and he snuggled into me like a koala.

He took a deep breath, let it out slowly, and was already sound asleep.

I WOKE up to find Lawson's side of the bed empty. Maybe that was the reason I woke up, I don't know. I heard him in the kitchen area, popping pain tablets from the blister pack. A quick check of my watch told me it was just past seven in the morning.

"Morning," I said. "Didn't realise it was so late." I'd normally be up for an hour by now.

He was standing at the glass sliding doors, looking out onto the morning, freshly showered and shaven, with a bottle of water in his hand. He was back in his sleep pants again, though, which told me he wasn't feeling too good. "Good morning," he replied, giving me a warm smile. "I was sick of lying down, sorry."

"Headache?"

He nodded.

"Anything I can do for you?"

He held his arms out, waiting until I fit myself right where he wanted me. He slipped his arms around my waist and let me pull him against me. I rubbed gentle circles on his back and he sighed. "There is something you can do for me."

"What's that?"

"I hope you don't think I'm being brazen by saying this, but you asked me once to move in with you and I foolishly turned you down. I thought I was doing the right thing, for us, by giving us some space while we found our feet together. And now I feel I may have missed my opportunity."

I pulled back so I could look into his eyes. "You want to move in with me?"

He made a face. "Yes. But it would only be proper if you asked me again. I can't bear the thought of imposing just because it's what I want now. I have no idea if you're still offering, but it would only feel right if you asked me again."

I was grinning. I couldn't help it. He was such a dork. "Lawson Gale, would you do me the honour of living with me?"

"And Rosemary?"

I amended my statement. "Lawson Gale, would you do me the most incredible honour of living with me *and Rosemary*?"

He smiled serenely. "There's nothing I want more. It would make my life perfecter, isn't that the word you used?"

"Yes! I told you it'd be a real word." I gave him a crushing hug, then remembered that he was unwell. I set him back on his feet. "Oh, sorry."

He laughed and patted his shirt down. "It's quite all right."

I cupped his face in both my hands. "Feel better now?"

"Perfecter." Lawson gave me a smile and leaned into me. "I don't want to be apart from you, not for anything. Not only did you save my life, but you've been everything and more while I've been ill. It's made me realise I don't want to waste another minute."

I kissed his forehead, then his lips, then pulled him in for a gentle hug. "Me too. I don't know what I'd have done if you didn't make it. Because truthfully, in the ambulance on the way to the hospital, I thought you were going to die." I shuddered at the memory. "I've never been so scared."

He tightened his hold on me. "I'm sorry you had to see

that. I can't even imagine what would have happened if it were you, Jack, that went down that embankment with those cane toads. I'd have never got you up the embankment, let alone carry you out of the forest." He pulled back and his frown was so utterly sad. "I can't even bear to think about it. And now we're two for two. First the bushfire, and now this. You've saved me twice."

I kissed him softly. "How about we don't try for a hat trick, okay?"

He finally laughed. "Well, I can attest to not trying to die again, that's for certain. But I'm sure there'll be other butterfly expeditions—"

I put my finger to his lip. "The correct answer is 'yes, Jack.'"

He chuckled. "I'd love some breakfast. But can we go to the restaurant? I don't want to be cooped up inside any longer than I need to be."

"Of course. Let me grab a quick shower."

Ten minutes later, I was ready to go, and Lawson had changed into some shorts and a shirt. He still looked tired, though I guessed the headache tablets had kicked in. "Ready?"

"Starving."

I chuckled, thinking that was his new state of being. We ate a breakfast of fruit, toast, and tea, and even though his energy levels had improved, he still tired easily. "How about we spend the morning lazing in the courtyard, then this afternoon, if you're up for it, we can go see Piers at the conservatory?"

He gave me a grateful smile. "Sounds perfect."

WHETHER HE FELT up to it or not, by mid-afternoon, Lawson was determined to visit Piers. I took his stubbornness as a sign that he was feeling better. Something I'd learned through all of this was that a sick Lawson was agreeable to almost everything. A feeling-better Lawson was getting back to his feisty self.

But I understood his frustration. No one liked being sick and dependent on someone else, so even though I thought he might be rushing it, I didn't want to dampen his mood. He simply washed two Advil down with some juice and grinned. "I'm good to go."

And going back to the conservatory did brighten his mood. As soon as we walked into the lab, Piers met us with an enthusiastic greeting. He put both hands on Lawson's shoulders and gave him the once over. "How are you feeling? You look better." Then Piers glanced at me. "He looks better, no?"

"He does. But he insisted on dropping by, and I know it'll be easier and quicker if I just agree and help him rather than argue, because we all know he's just going to do it himself anyway."

Lawson considered this for a moment, then conceded. "True."

Piers laughed. "Ah, it is good to have you both here. Come and look."

It almost looked like a different lab. There were charts, folders, spreadsheets, data, laptops, and a smartboard, and Piers showed Lawson each one, in turn, pointing out the data Lawson had collated, and they discussed numbers and pH levels and bio-somethings, while I didn't even pretend to understand.

"Isn't it fascinating?" Piers asked with a flourish. Lawson quickly agreed, and I nodded. Though what was really fascinating was the difference in attitude in Piers. Where before he was frustrated and angry at getting nowhere, now he was excited and driven by results. If I had wondered at Piers' ability to keep the ball rolling, I certainly didn't now. He was all over it.

"We're expecting a good wet season," Piers said. "First decent one in four years. It will flush out existing pools and toxicity levels. So we should see significant improvement in the Ulysses environment in the next few seasons. In the meantime, we're considering special gardens and plantations specific to the doughwood. We'll have safeguards, of course, now we know the cane toad tadpole is to blame. Thanks to you, Lawson.

"And we've presented our findings to the environmental departments in Papua New Guinea, the Solomons, and Indonesia. Though Indonesia has had good rainfall, so they're not seeing the results we have. It seems we might be able to secure some breeding pairs from them once we are sure we have resolved our situation the best we can."

"That is terrific news!" Lawson said.

"Yes. Come see this," Piers added quickly.

I put my hand up like a stop sign. "I'll go find Gary and sort out the camping gear. You two will be a while here, no doubt." They both nodded like it was a given. "I'll be back soon. And Piers? Would you mind getting Lawson a stool to sit on or something?"

Lawson gave me a half-irritated, half-thankful scowl. Piers threw his hands up like he couldn't believe he didn't think of that. "Yes! Of course, silly me. Where are my manners?"

I left them to it and went in search of Gary. He'd been kind enough to pack up all our camping gear that we'd had to leave behind in the middle of the forest. I caught him as he was zooming past on a quad runner with some kind of wood and tarp contraption on the back. He pulled up to a stop as soon as he saw me.

"Hey," he said warmly. "How's Lawson?"

"Better. Recovering, though it's slower than he'd like."

"I bet. I've got all your camping gear back in my shed. I can grab it for you now if you like? All the tubs and work gear I left with Piers." He nodded in the general direction of the conservatory.

"Well, I have no real way of getting it all back to Tassie anyway, plus I've got all my own camping gear. Could anyone around here use it?"

"Sure they could!" he replied brightly. "We have camping expeditions into the forest with tourists, school groups, research students. I'm sure it'll get put to good use, if you're sure?"

"Positive." Then I took a closer look at the weird looking apparatus he was taking somewhere. "What is that thing? Are they buoys?"

He snorted and got off the quad runner. "Yep. I got thinkin' about those tadpoles, you know, the ones we have in the water tank for the orchard filtration system."

I nodded. "And?"

"And I got to lookin' on some cane toad site online. A team in Brissie designed a kind of funnel trap and a bait that attracts the tadpoles. Some kind of pheromone thing. Anyway, I contacted 'em and got approval through my boss to get some of the bait. But I rigged this trap up myself after looking at theirs. Wasn't too hard." He held it up and showed me the underneath. It was indeed some kind of funnel trap that sat on the water surface. "Little buggers go in here and can't get out. They reckon they caught tens of thousands in a just a few days."

"That's awesome!" I said, looking the device over. "Lawson would love it!"

Gary smiled proudly. "Guess it certainly can't hurt. Who knows? If we try it here, it might help this team in Brisbane with a trial."

"That's incredible," I said. I liked Gary. We were a lot alike. Both outdoorsy, better with our hands than with our brains. "I better get back. But hey, if you're ever down south and want to see how the Tasmanian Parks and Wildlife do their thing, I'd love to show you around. I really appreciate everything you've done for us."

"Will do," he said. He shook my hand, got back on the quad runner, and went on his way.

When I got back to the lab, Lawson was sitting on the stool, and he and Piers were both studying a laptop screen filled with tables of numbers. Lawson looked up and smiled, and I rubbed his back. "How're you feeling?" The fact he was sitting on the stool while Piers was standing told me enough.

"Okay. Tired."

I kissed the side of his head. "Just spoke to Gary. He showed me a funnel trap he made himself for the retention tank at the orchard. There's some kind of bait he found online that attracts the tadpoles and kills them."

"Yes," Lawson said. He gestured to the screen. "We were just looking at that. Can you believe the bait they're testing is from the cane toad's own poison?"

I barked out a laugh. "Actually, I can believe that. I've seen what that poison can do."

Lawson gave me a sad smile. "Indeed."

"Apparently the pheromone they extract attracts only the cane toad tadpole, not any other frog species," Piers went on to say.

Lawson still hadn't stopped looking at me. "Did you get everything sorted with Gary?"

I rubbed his back again. "I did." He was still tired, I could tell. "You ready to go?"

He gave me a small nod. "Yes. I can't believe how utterly exhausted I am. We did nothing but lie about reading all morning." Then he seemed to reconsider what he said. "Well, Jack read. I mostly slept."

I rubbed his back some more. "The doc said it'll take a while. You need to take it easy."

The look he shot me said *I am taking it easy*, and Piers chuckled. "Well, Lawson and Jack, I must say it has been a true joy to have you both here. I owe you both an immeasurable debt. I hate to think where we'd be if you hadn't made the connection between the toxin bufadienolides and bioaccumulation and transference."

"It's my absolute pleasure," Lawson said. "And I have no regrets about not staying on." Before Piers could be offended, Lawson added, "Because I know it's in very capable hands."

We bid Piers farewell, with him promising to email Lawson often with updates, or to call if he needed, and we headed back to the hotel. Lawson leaned his head against the headrest and smiled sleepily at me. "No regrets on not staying?" I asked.

He shook his head a little. "None."

I grinned at him as I drove. "Me either."

"I miss Rosemary. I miss the quiet of your house, the smell of your bed. I want to go home, Jack."

I took his hand and gave it a squeeze. "Tomorrow. By this time tomorrow, you'll be on the sofa with Rosemary at your side, and I'll be in the kitchen cooking you my Nonna's lasagne."

"Sounds perfect," he mumbled, almost asleep in the car. "So tired."

When we got back to the hotel, I managed to get him into bed, took his shoes off, pulled his trousers off, but left his shirt and undies on. I pulled up the blanket, kissed his forehead. "Love you," I whispered and let him sleep.

BY THE TIME we got all of Lawson's tubs and work gear organised for freight back to Tasmania and then into the airport ourselves, I could tell he was already lagging. We'd only been up for a few hours and I'd done all the packing and lifting, but he was still weary. "Want me to get you a courtesy wheelchair?"

He shot me a horrified look. "No! Of course not!"

When we boarded the plane, he sank into his seat and snoozed for most of the flight. But when we arrived in Melbourne, he was having trouble staying awake. "Want a wheelchair now?" I asked. "We have to walk to the other end of the terminal, Lawson. It's not worth ending up back in hospital, is it?"

He pouted but didn't argue, and that was answer enough for me. I asked a stewardess if we could please have a wheelchair, and without any trouble, we had one. I pushed him through the terminal to our gate, and he never said a thing. When we finally took our seats on the plane to Launceston, he let out a heavy sigh.

"You okay?" I asked.

He blinked slowly, barely awake. "Yeah."

I took hold of his hand. "Remember the first time we met, it was on this flight. Melbourne to Launceston."

He smiled. "Yes, you laughed at me, then trampled me into the aisle."

I barked out a laugh. "I did not! Anyway, I seem to remember you calling me a serial killer."

He closed his eyes and squeezed my hand. "The foundation of all perfect relationships."

I chuckled and was going to say something else, but he was already asleep.

THERE REALLY IS nothing like coming home. Even the biting Tasmanian cold didn't dampen my spirits.

Lawson snoozed the entire drive from Launceston to Scottsdale. When I'd asked him if he wanted to go to his place or mine, his answer was immediate. "Yours. Ours. Take me home, Jack."

My heart almost beat right out of my chest.

And my smile got bigger as I turned down Stanning Road. I was taking him home—mine, his, ours. We'd worry about getting his things moved later, but for now, he needed rest and recuperation. And if he stayed at home, then Rosemary and I could look after him.

It seemed Remmy had other ideas.

As my house came into view, so did four cars, all parked in my front yard. Remmy and Nico's car was there, and I knew she had to be the one behind it.

I drove up to the house and pulled on the handbrake. I knew she only had the best of intentions, but Lawson really wasn't up for a welcoming committee. At least they'd have the fire going, I reasoned. I climbed out of my ute and walked around to Lawson's door. He was still asleep, so I gently shook his arm. "Hey, Lawson, baby, we're home."

He startled awake and looked bleary eyed at the house. With my hand under his elbow, I helped him out and up the front porch steps. It was only then he seemed to notice the cars in the front yard, and as I opened the door, a loud and warm 'welcome home' cried out from the lounge room.

God, everyone was there. Rosemary, of course. Remmy, Nico, Luka. My mum and step-dad, my sisters, and Lawson's parents. A huge sign stuck to the wall read "Welcome home and thanks for not dying" which made me laugh.

Lawson was shocked, to say the least, but he was all smiles as his mum and dad hugged him. Hyacinth had her hands to his face, but I was distracted by Remmy almost tackling me into a fierce hug. "Oh my God, Jack. Is he okay?"

"He's fine, Remmy, thank you. Travelling has just taken it out of him, that's all."

I turned to find Lawson bending down and giving Rosemary a half pat, half cuddle, and she was wriggling herself crazy. I gave her a scratch behind the ear. "Hey, you're supposed to greet me first," I pretended to rouse on her.

Lawson gave me a smile. "She loves me."

I slid my arm around his back. "Yes, she does."

Then Lawson's parents hugged me. "Thank you for everything," his mum said.

"It was nothing," I replied humbly.

His dad put his hand on my shoulder. "It was everything."

Then I noticed my parents and sisters watching. I rubbed Lawson's back. "Come on, I want you to meet my folks."

Lawson didn't budge. He mumbled, "I'm not really dressed appropriately to be meeting your family."

He was wearing his navy trousers and a pale blue button-down shirt and looked more than fine to me. "You look great." He made a face. I leaned in and whispered, "They'll love you no matter what you wear."

Reluctantly, he let me lead him over to where my family were standing back. "Mum, Dad, this is Lawson Gale. Lawson, this is Robert and Katherine Brighton. And my sisters, April and Poppy, who you've spoken with on the phone."

My dad, or technically my step-father, but he was the only dad I really knew, was first to reply. He shook Lawson's hand. "We've heard so much about you, it's good to finally meet you, son."

"So very nice to finally meet you," Mum said, taking his hands. "We heard about how sick you got in Queensland, and Remmy said she was having a little welcome home party. I hope you don't mind?"

Lawson quickly answered. "No, I don't mind at all. I'm very glad to meet you both. I'm just sorry I'm not exactly dressed for first impressions." He patted down his hair, which was a nervous thing he hadn't done in a while. "It's been quite a long day."

I took his hand. "Excuse us for a second," I said, leading him to the hall. "We'll be right back."

There was silence behind us, but Remmy saved the situation. "Right, then. Pot of tea is on. Who wants cake?"

I took Lawson into my bedroom and sat him down on the edge of the bed. "What are you doing?" he asked, looking up at me.

"You're not comfortable," I stated. "Take your shirt off."

His eyes bugged out, but I went to my wardrobe and pulled out one of his shirts. I handed it to him. "Here. Put this on." Then I went to my dresser drawers and took out one of his bow ties. "You'll feel much better if you're dressed the way you feel most comfortable."

His eyes got glassy, and for a moment I thought he might cry. "Thank you." He slowly pulled on the shirt and did up the buttons. It was just plain white with long sleeves, but it was freshly pressed. He took a little longer to finish buttoning up, as though his arms were tired, so I popped his collar up and he let his arms fall to his sides while I tried to tie his bow tie. It had been years, and I was never really any good at them. It was a yellow bow tie, one he'd left here ages ago. "I wondered where I left this one," he said quietly.

When I met his eyes, he was staring up at me with such love. I folded his collar down, leaned in, and kissed him. "I kinda suck at doing ties of any kind," I said, "and it's crooked, and one side is bigger than the other, just a little bit, but still. Not exactly symmetrical like how you do them."

He stood up, his eyes never leaving mine. "I don't care. It's perfect."

"You uh, haven't seen it."

"I don't need to."

"You sure you feel okay?"

He nodded. "Yes. Tired, but otherwise fine. We best not keep them waiting. And I believe there's tea."

I kissed him one more time for good luck. "And cake."

I took his hand and led him back out to where our friends and family were sitting around the dining table, drinking tea. I eyed the almost-gone cake. "There better be some of that left," I said.

"Hummingbird cake," Remmy said, quickly cutting me a huge slice. "Your favourite."

I pulled out a chair at the table for Lawson to sit on, which he took with a shy smile. I only realised a little too late that it was in between my mother and his. I gave his shoulder a squeeze and pulled out a stool from under the kitchen bench. Remmy handed me the plate of cake, but I needed to grab a spoon, and Remmy quickly cornered me in the kitchen.

She looked panic stricken. "I didn't realise he was still so ill. He looks awful. If I'd known... Jack, I'm sorry. This party is probably the last thing he wanted..."

"He's okay. Just tired. Well, he's better than he was, that's for sure. And this party is perfect, thank you."

She frowned. "How did your first holiday together go, apart from the almost dying part? I mean, first holidays away together are a make or break thing..."

"He wants to move in with me."

Remmy bit back a squeal but still had to cover her mouth. "Oh my God," she said from behind her hand. "I'm so happy for you."

"Me too."

Then I heard Lawson's mum say, "Oh, Lawson, honey, seriously, you should have studied medicine and not be out traipsing through the wilderness almost getting yourself killed by bushfires or toxic wildlife."

His dad laughed. "If he did study medicine, Hyacinth, he'd be off in some remote part of the globe helping village children in Peru. Or Cambodia. Or Uganda."

I couldn't help but laugh. "That's so true. He totally would be."

Lawson sipped his tea just as Rosemary padded over to him. She knew better than to approach the dining table, but I couldn't bring myself to rebuke her. She rested her head on his thigh, as though she somehow knew he wasn't feeling too great. He stroked her forehead and she closed her eyes, and I found myself smiling at them. Remmy nudged my side and gave me a knowing smirk before she reclaimed her seat at the table. Luca clambered all over her lap and I ate my cake while everyone chatted and talked, told stories and laughed.

My sisters claimed Lawson for their own, and I could tell by the way they smiled at him that he had totally charmed them. My mum watched on fondly, and with her cup of tea in hand, she stood beside my stool at the kitchen bench. "He's lovely," she said.

"He is."

She sighed contentedly. "I'm so glad you found him."

"Well, I was watching him when he slid down the embankment. I didn't exactly have to find him."

She rubbed my hand. "No, Jack. I mean, I'm glad you found someone who makes you so happy."

"Oh." I pretended I wasn't embarrassed. I met her gaze so she could read the seriousness in mine. "He does, Mum. He's moving in with me."

She gave me an eye-crinkling smile. "Well, it's always good to live with someone, find out all their bad habits before you get married."

I choked on my tea, and we caught ourselves a few glances from around the table. I dabbed a serviette to my mouth. "Jeez, Mum."

She simply smiled in that knowing way mothers do. "I can see how you are with him, love. The way you look at him, and how he looks at you. And his parents are lovely. Having met them before meeting him, he wasn't at all what I expected."

I chuckled. "He's not what I expected either."

She squeezed my hand. "Hey, Jack," Poppy called out. "I was just telling Lawson of that time in high school—"

"Please don't," I said, cutting her off. "Whatever story you're about to tell, I'd rather you just stop right there."

April clapped her hands together. "Aww, come on Jackie, it was funny."

I sighed. "Please don't call me that." It was then I looked at Lawson; he was fighting to keep his eyelids open. Mum saw it the same time I did, then Lawson's dad did too.

I put my cup down and was just about to go to him when my mum stopped me. "Okay, well, we better get going," she said. "We've got the drive back to Hobart ahead of us."

"Oh yes, we should be going too," Lawson's dad said, giving a subtle nod to Lawson. "You boys have had a long day."

Remmy agreed, and I walked her, Nico, and Luca to the door. "I'm sorry, Jack," she said. "I feel so bad. The poor guy!"

I pulled her in for a hug. "Thank you. And no more apologies. The welcome home party was lovely, and the *thanks for not dying part* was a nice touch."

She gave me a shrug and half a smile. "I thought so too."

I waved them off with a laugh and a promise to call into the bakery tomorrow.

I hugged my mum and dad and sisters and thanked them for making the effort to come visit. "We'll come to Hobart next time. I promise."

Mum hugged me the hardest, and Dad clapped my shoulder. "You need to look after him," he ordered with a smile. "Poor kid looks beat."

"I will."

Lawson thanked them for coming, telling them he was very pleased to meet them, but his blinks were getting longer and longer. His parents left the same time as mine did, but they were staying in town and flying back to Melbourne the next afternoon.

I had no doubt we'd see them again bright and early but didn't begrudge them for wanting to spend some time with Lawson. "We'll bring out breakfast," Darren offered.

"I'd love that," I answered. "We haven't had a chance to grab milk or bread or anything really."

So with plans made, they drove off, leaving the house in a silence that felt like a comfy blanket. I took Lawson to bed, undressed him, and tucked him in. It was still too early for me to fall asleep, so I did some tidying up, some laundry, then planted myself on the floor with Rosemary.

"It's good to be home, hey, girl?"

She replied with a tongue-lolling smile and a wag of her tail.

"You want Lawson to come live with us?"

She wiggled her butt.

"You'll have two daddies, huh? How does that sound?"

She huffed, and I swear she was smiling.

"Yeah, sounds pretty good to me too."

CHAPTER THIRTEEN

LAWSON

I WOKE up to the smell of food and the sound of voices and laughter. I had no idea what time it was, and I took a moment to assess how I felt. There was an ever present ache in my head, like a band that tightened inside my skull. I was still bone weary, which was absurd because I'd just slept for God knows how long.

I sat up and put my feet to the floor, giving myself some time to adjust. I reached for my phone to find it was almost eight. Bother. I'd slept for... I couldn't even remember what time I went to bed.

I pulled on my trousers, relieved myself in the bathroom, brushed my teeth and washed my face, then went in search of Jack. I found him in the kitchen with my parents, laughing about something to do with stewed fruit. I'm not sure I wanted to know.

Jack got to his feet as soon as he saw me. "Oh, you're awake! Want some tea? Your mum and dad brought out some of Remmy's breakfast specials and some bread and milk, so I can make you some toast?"

I gave him a smile just before Mum put her hand to my face. "You look so much better."

"I feel better," I admitted. I looked over her shoulder to Jack. "Tea, please."

It was lovely to spend some time with my parents, it really was. They were worried about me, as were Paterson and Mackellar. And I think they had a newfound adoration of Jack after he'd carried me out of the rainforest. They liked him before, but now I highly doubted he could ever do wrong in their eyes.

He doted on me, making sure I had everything I needed. When my parents left, he put me on the couch with snacks, drinks, phone and laptop, books, TV remote, all within reach. Rosemary sat by my side the entire day, the fire well stocked and blazing, while Jack went into town to catch up on a bit of work, call in to see Remmy, and grab some groceries. I only dozed once or twice.

On the second day, Jack left me in bed, and I spent the day a little more upright and only dozed once. I also notified the real estate agent of my intent to vacate my rental, which was an overwhelmingly wonderful feeling.

I couldn't even remember why I ever thought not living with him was a good idea.

It was unusual, though, being in Jack's home without him. All his belongings, all his personal effects, his entire life was in this house. It was a curious feeling, being surrounded by him but not having him here.

He did leave work a little early so he could be home with me, though after two weeks off it was hardly feasible. But he was adamant. He was also devoted to my wellbeing, my recuperation, though I couldn't convince him that I was well enough for sex.

I was feeling better every hour, and he was attentive to

my every need. Except that one.

By the fourth day, I'd tended to all my emails, I'd spoken to Professor Tillman on the phone, and to Piers, who both assured me all was going well. I'd sat by the *Bursaria spinosa* we'd planted near the rosemary, in hopes of spotting a Tillman Copper. Not that I expected to, especially in winter when butterflies were more docile, but as a lepidopterist, I hoped. The shrub had taken well, the ants were building a nice nest underneath it... but no butterflies. Yet.

I decided I'd cook dinner for Jack and settled on lamb souvlaki and couscous salad. I'd also decided I'd had enough of his abstinence, so I was freshly showered, wearing my normal trousers and shirt, but added the bow tie and suspenders. Because, well, because Jack had a thing for suspenders...

He greeted me with a warm, humming kiss. "Something smells great."

"Me or the food?"

"Both."

"It's almost done."

"Good, because I'm starving. How are you feeling?"

"Better. I didn't nap at all today."

Jack grinned. "Are these"—he trailed his fingers over the suspenders, over my collarbone—"for any reason in particular?"

My hopes soared, and those elusive butterflies that only existed in his presence flooded my belly. "Is that smile indicative of your willingness and intent to bed me later?"

He gave me a blank stare. "What?"

"You won't touch me. You won't have sex with me."

"Because you're unwell, Lawson. No other reason."

"But I'm not unwell anymore."

He put his fingers to my chin and lifted my face so he

could stare into my eyes. "My abstinence is not a reflection of anything but your physical wellbeing. You know I love you. You know I love being intimate with you." His eyes flashed with a spark. "And wearing suspenders is a low blow. You know how much I love taking them off you."

I smiled victoriously. "That was the reason I wore them."

He kissed me briefly, then put his finger to my lips. "Dinner first, then you can tell me about your day, and then we'll see if you feel up to it."

I never thought I'd be one to feel antsy without sex. Lord knows I'd endured dry spells to rival the Sahara. But I needed him in ways I'd not needed anyone before. Yes, I needed him emotionally, but I also needed him physically as well.

I was craving him.

"What is it?" he murmured, cradling my face in his hands.

"I need to feel connected to you. I thought there were always two different kinds of connections: physical and emotional, but I've just realised that when you make love to me, I get both. I need to feel that. I need to feel reconnected and I need you to..."

He pressed himself against me and he whispered in my ear, "You need me to what?"

I closed my eyes and spoke the words against his neck. "To make me yours again. I feel disengaged since the accident, detached almost. But when you're inside me, I feel... centred."

He sucked back a breath. "Lawson?" His voice was rough and thick with desire.

"Yes."

"Turn the hotplates off." I grinned and he bit my bottom

lip, gently pulling it between his teeth. "And don't be so smug about it."

I quickly shut dinner off, and when I turned around, Jack held his hand out. Without a word, he led me to his bedroom, our bedroom, and stopped. He stood right up close and slipped a finger under one of my suspenders and slid it off my shoulder. He licked his lips, his eyes smouldered, and the butterflies in my belly took flight. With just as much dedication, he slid the other suspender from my shoulder and watched it fall to my side. Then he tilted my head back, then ghosted his lips across mine. "I need to use the bathroom. Don't go anywhere."

It took me a second to realise he'd gone. I'm not sure I'd breathed the entire time and my head buzzed. I undressed quickly, leaving my clothes in a pile on the floor, too impatient to fold neatly. I took the lube from the bedside drawer and climbed on the bed, laying on my belly. Without waiting for him to return—I simply couldn't wait a second longer—I slicked my own fingers and slid them along my arse crack, over my hole, and pushed one fingertip inside myself.

I heard Jack's gasp from the bedroom door. "Lawson." His voice was strained.

"I can't wait. I need this, Jack. I need you."

I heard the rustle of fabric as he undressed. The zipper undoing sent a thrill through me, and I raised my hips and pushed a second fingertip inside myself.

"Fuck," he rasped out.

I turned my head at the sound and saw him naked, staring at me, stroking himself. "Jack, please."

He smirked and knelt on the bed. "Remove your hand," he ordered gruffly.

I did, and he took my leg closest to him and manoeuvred

me so I was on my back instead. Then, still gripping my ankle, he pulled me closer to him so he was now between my legs. "I need to see your face," he murmured. "I need to kiss you while I fill you."

My cock jerked at his words and he smiled. I wrapped my fingers around my shaft and Jack's nostrils flared. I let my eyes wander down to the hair on his chest, down to his almost-defined abs, and further down to his proud erection. His cock was fully engorged, the cockhead purple, precome at the tip.

He slid his huge hands around my thighs and lifted my legs toward my chest, then leaned over me so his lips were almost touching mine. His thick and heavy cock slid along my perineum, teasing. I tried to push onto him, but he held me still. "Jack, I've not the patience for teasing right now."

"I can tell you're feeling better," he said with a smirk. "Because you're back to being feisty and bossy in bed." He gripped his cock and pressed against my hole, but didn't push in. He loved driving me to the brink and never seemed satisfied until I cursed and demanded he do certain things to my body.

"Jack, I swear, if you don't fuck me right now."

His eyes flashed with triumph. "You'll what?"

I reached down between us and slid my fingers past my balls. "I'll do it myself."

Jack gripped my hand and pinned it to the mattress by my head, and in one thrust, he pushed into me.

He was bigger than I'd remembered.

"Fuck," I gasped, blinking and trying to breathe.

Jack's eyes smouldered. His voice was gruff, his lips against mine. "Is that what you wanted?"

I nodded and groaned as he settled himself inside as far as he could go. As far as I could take him. He let go of my hand and gripped my hair instead. He kissed me as he pulled back, almost all the way, then slowly slid back in. Over and over.

It was everything I needed. Feeling owned by him, claimed and taken. There could be no doubt I was his when he took me like this.

He broke the kiss, trailing his lips down my jaw to my neck. And he never stopped fucking, reminding me with every thrust that I was his, and he was mine. He increased his tempo, speeding closer and closer to the precipice. "Lawson," he rasped. "Need you to come." I shook my head, and he pulled back so he could look into my eyes. "I need you to come first." He thrust slower now, as if he wanted to stop but couldn't.

"Not this time. I just need you to come inside me."

He moaned and he closed his eyes, and I could feel him swell deep within me. He put one hand at the top of my head, his other cupped my jaw, and he arched fully with a guttural moan as he came.

He surged inside me, spilling his seed, and he cried out with a final shudder as his orgasm subsided. He collapsed on top of me but nuzzled into my neck. "My God," he mumbled. Once his breaths had calmed, he kissed that spot below my ear that made me shiver. He kissed up my jaw to my mouth. His eyes were glazed over, sated and happy. "Feel better?"

I took stock of every inch of my body, my mind, giving a little roll of my spine. "I feel superb."

He kissed me with smiling lips. "I can tell. You're almost purring."

I chuckled. "Helps that you're still inside me."

He kissed me and rolled his hips. "I never want to leave."

"Then don't."

He ran his thumb across my cheek. "Are you not tired?"

I shook my head. "Not really."

"Good. Because you didn't get off, so there needs to be a round two."

I hummed, liking the sound of that very much. "We never did test our theory on bioaccumulation."

Jack laughed and slowly slipped out of my body, quickly wrapping me up in his arms instead. "I'm going to need about twenty minutes and some food."

"Should we venture out to the kitchen?"

"If we have to."

Neither of us moved, just enjoying the peaceful moment between us. "Thank you," I said eventually. "For not denying me. I felt quite out of sorts, and it didn't really occur to me what it was. But I needed this intimacy between us. It was rather difficult to articulate, but I just needed to be yours again. And you did exactly that. So, thank you."

"You were out of sorts. But you feel okay now?"

I nodded and kissed his chest. "Much better."

Jack sighed. It was a contented sound with a hint of understanding. He gave me a hard squeeze and another kiss to the side of my head. "Just so you know, Lawson, my love, you are mine, and I am yours. But if you ever need reminding, I won't ever deny you." He pulled back so he could put his hand to my cheek and kiss me.

"I love you, Jack. Now and forever."

He smiled. "Thank you."

I kissed him softly. "Let me get you some dinner, then we can further our research on biotransference and accumulation."

Jack laughed. "All the bio-somethings there are?"

"All of them."

———

TEN MINUTES LATER, I'd finished cooking off dinner, resurrected the couscous and served two plates to the table. I went back to the kitchen for a bottle of water and two glasses when Jack came in from being out the back with Rosemary. She'd needed to go, so he'd followed her to grab some more firewood, which he stacked next to the fire. Then he walked over to me, windswept and his nose an adorable red from the cold, with a sprig of rosemary and a wild daisy from the grass. He slid them into a small white vase and presented them to me with a proud smile. "For you. It's been too long since I offered flowers."

I took the vase gratefully. "They're perfect." I put them to my nose and inhaled everything that reminded me of Jack—earth and outdoors, sweet and unpretentious, and all that was good in the world—and smiled up at him. "Thank you."

We sat at the table and ate our dinner, with the small vase between us, and Rosemary asleep in front of the roaring fire. If perfect was a moment personified, this was it, right here.

And when we were done, Jack took my hand and led me back to bed. I was sleepy, not in an unwell-exhausted way, but in a warm and happy way. Jack lay me out on the bed and showed me every way he adored me, and I'd almost felt foolish for needing his reaffirmation of how I belonged to him earlier. He made those butterflies in my belly take flight and dance on every nerve ending; he made my heart morph into something that would belong to him always.

And I'd never doubt again.

I LEFT Professor Tillman's butterfly house in Launceston after spending the day with the Tillman Copper's latest newly emerged kaleidoscope, with a printed off email in hand, and headed straight for Jack's office in Scottsdale.

Karen greeted me first. "Lawson, so good to see you!" She looked flustered. "But Jack's not here."

"Oh, is he out in the field or something?"

"Um, uh." She was a terrible liar. "He's gone home for the day, actually."

"Oh, was he unwell?"

She side-eyed me. "Not exactly."

I wasn't quite sure what to say to that. "Okay, well then, I'll just meet him there. I guess."

She grimaced, then tried to smile. "Okay." As I walked out, I could already hear her clambering to pick up the phone.

Well. That was very odd.

I drove home, wondering what on earth Jack had gone home for and why Karen was being so secretive. Jack's ute was parked where it always was beside the house, and I pulled in behind it and went inside.

Jack met me in the lounge room like he'd raced to greet me. Rosemary skidded to a stop beside him, both looking ridiculously happy.

"Good afternoon, Doctor."

I smiled at his greeting. Since I'd gained my doctorate, he'd taken to addressing me as such. I think he got off on it, to be honest. "Hi. I called into your office, but Karen told me you were here."

"Oh yes, she just called..." He swallowed hard when he'd realised he'd said too much. His ability to lie rivalled Karen's. His eyes went to the papers I was holding. "What you got there?"

"Well... it's a letter from the New South Wales Lepidopterist Society..."

"And?"

"It's more of a formal request, actually."

"A request?"

"Yes, you see, they read my journal entry on the Ulysses last month, and of course they know of my work with the Tillman Copper."

"And?"

"And there's a butterfly, the *Pasma tasmanicus* or the Two Spotted Grass Skipper, as it's more commonly known, and it's typically found at altitudes such as the Blue Mountains or Mount Kosciuszko. It's bivoltine, however, researchers are claiming there's been no summer brood this year."

Jack stared then nodded slowly. "And they want you to look into it?"

I smiled and handed the letter over so he could read it. "Yes, hence the formal request."

He read the first line. "Doctor Gale." He looked up at me. "Sounds formal."

Yes, there was definitely a doctor kink.

He went back to reading and I waited for him to finish. He looked up and tilted his head. "Did you call them?"

"Yes."

"And? When did they want you to go?"

"As it's summer and the wildflowers are in full bloom, it would make sense to go soon. Winter would be redundant, as the snow over Kosciuszko would make things rather difficult. Especially if we were to camp out."

"We?"

"Of course."

His lips twitched before becoming a smile. "Really?"

"Yes. After the last few incidents, I don't think my parents would approve of me going alone."

A huff of laughter escaped him. "That's probably true. I don't want to think about what trouble you could find in the Snowy Mountains by yourself."

I rolled my eyes. "I thought with your position with the national parks, we might gain special access."

"Ah, so you're only inviting me for my perks, huh?"

I chuckled. "Well, yes. And your ability to save my life if needed."

"Well, there is that."

He handed the letter back to me. "I could put in for some time off. I mean, the survival of a species might very well depend on it."

I stepped in and leaned up on my toes so I could kiss him. "You're wonderful."

He buzzed with a cute little smile. "I know."

"So, do you want to tell me what you and Rosemary were doing outside?"

His eyes widened. "What?"

"You both came inside as I pulled up. And I assume it's what Karen failed to lie about when I called in."

He took a deep breath and let it out slowly. "It isn't quite ready yet, but I wasn't expecting you until around five."

My curiosity was piqued. "What is it?"

"Close your eyes."

I did, and he took me by the hand and led me out the back. I was confused as to where he'd taken me because I thought we'd gone right, but we should have run into a fence by now. But I trusted him so I kept my eyes closed. When I was in the spot Jack deemed correct, he stopped me. "Okay, open your eyes."

We were standing to the right of the house in the next paddock, where the fence had been taken down. There were four wooden pegs in the ground with string lines between the pegs, outlining a rather large rectangle. "I wasn't finished pegging it out when you got here."

Was he building another house? "What is it?"

He put his hand up in a one-sec notion, raced over to the back of the house, and came back with some papers. He handed them to me.

It was a legal document with our local council insignia blazoned across the top, with the words Development Application in bold.

The applicant — Mr Jack Brighton.

Proposed Development — a butterfly house.

Status — approved.

My gaze went from the papers in my hand to Jack. "A butterfly house?"

He nodded. "Your very own."

I walked into the outlined footprint of the butterfly

house and looked around. My heart swelled with emotions I couldn't name, my eyes burned with tears. The butterflies in my belly flooded my throat and I couldn't speak. It was the most incredible gesture, the most extraordinary gift. Tears spilled down my cheeks, and Jack was suddenly alarmed.

"Is it okay? If you don't like it..."

I laughed, because how on earth could I not like this? "It's perfect," I tried to say through my tears.

"Oh, thank God," he said, laughing with relief. He threw his arms around me and pulled me in for a hug. "You like it?"

"I love it. It's more than I could ever ask for. *You* are more than I could ever ask for."

"I had some help with the design I submitted. Warner, of course, and Piers too, they both drew up their ideal designs and helped me with requirements. We'll need to get a specialist architect, I'd reckon, but the plans I submitted are approved pending proper—"

"Marry me."

He stared, his mouth open. "What?"

"Marry me," I repeated before I could lose my nerve. He was still staring, so I explained, "Jack, there are species of *Lepidoptera* all over this world, but there are none—none—like those I experience when I'm with you. You are quite possibly the most perfect man, with the kindest heart, and you make me strive to be a better person. And this here—" I looked around us, the Tasmanian countryside, Rosemary off sniffing around the garden, this perfect piece of life. "It's everything I want for the rest of my life. I want to grow old with you, right here. Marry me, Jack. Please."

Jack put his fingers under my chin, and taking a deep breath, he leaned in and fluttered his eyelashes along my cheekbone before kissing me softly on the lips. He shivered, and when he opened his eyes, they were glassy with tears, and he nodded. He could barely speak. "Yes."

EPILOGUE

JACK

Two years later

IT WAS a glorious Tasmanian summer day, barely a cloud in the sky. I was at Remmy's helping her with the finishing touches on the menu because Lawson insisted we had to spend the day apart.

It wasn't right to see each other before the wedding, he'd said.

He was probably right, not that I was superstitious at all, and truthfully neither was he. But it gave us some time to spend with our families before the big event. My sisters and parents were with me at Remmy's. Lawson's parents and his brother and sister and their partners were at home putting the final touches in.

Not that they needed to. Everything was perfect.

We'd spent the better part of two years making sure everything was spot on.

It was really a very simple affair. Uncomplicated and perfect, Lawson said.

"This is the sweetest menu I've put together," Remmy said as she took the last batch of pastries out of her oven. She had done the majority of the baking at the bakery but she was never happy unless she had extras and a few special bits and pieces.

"What do you mean?" Mum asked. "I thought Jack said it was a simple menu."

"Didn't he tell you?" Poppy chimed in. Poppy was sitting at the dining table while April was doing her hair, curling or straightening, I couldn't tell the difference, to be honest.

Mum frowned. "Tell me what?"

"Jack and Lawson wanted to replicate the menu of their first date," Poppy said, fluttering her eyelashes. "Such romantics."

"It was special to us," I added, needing to defend myself. "And it's not *simple*, it's just not fancy fine dining. It's what Remmy put together when I said I'd met a guy I wanted to impress." I could feel myself blush, so I stopped talking.

"It is sweet," Remmy said. "And perfect for you both." But then she turned total traitor and blabbed to my entire family. "It was so cute. He set up a table for two with a little vase of flowers in the bakery after closing time, and I made a basket of things for them to share. Lawson was swept off his feet; never stood a chance, the poor boy."

"It wasn't flowers. It was a flow*er*. Single. Not plural."

"Getting a single flower sometimes means more than getting a whole bouquet," April said with a wistful sigh.

"And those are the flowers they're having for their wedding, in their lapels, on the table," Remmy added, throwing me right under the bus. "There were five dates, five different types of flowers."

My mum put her hand on her heart. "Awwww."

April counted on her fingers. "White Milligan's daisy. Jasmine. Rosemary. Yellow daisy, and the *Bursaria*, of course."

"I know!" Poppy cried. "It's like the sweetest thing ever."

"Are you guys done?" I asked. Pleaded. Whatever. "Anyway, the *Bursaria* wasn't from a date. It's the shrub Lawson planted at the side of our house. It's a wedding. It's supposed to be romantic."

Just then, the front door opened and Dad came in first, followed by Nico and Luca, with a freshly groomed Rosemary.

"She wanted to roll in the duck poo," Luca announced with a grin.

"Almost did too," Dad added. "Walked out of the groomer's place, took three steps, and aimed right for a big streak of—"

Mum put up her hand. "We get it."

I bent down and gave Rosemary a pat and ruffled the fur on her forehead. "You look real pretty, Miss Rosemary. Got a big day today, huh?"

She gave me a tongue-lolling grin then proceeded to sniff out Remmy's cooking in the kitchen. Yeah, she knew who had the good stuff. She padded over to Remmy, sat down in front of her, and waited for a fresh-baked treat. Remmy made baby talk to her but promptly rewarded her for being a such a good girl.

My dad, or step-dad, but really my only dad, nudged my elbow with his. He gave me a small, patient smile. "You ready?"

He wasn't asking if I was ready, like showered and shaved. He was asking if I was ready to be married, if I was ready to change my life forever, from *me* to *we*. "I really am."

Nico clapped my shoulder. "Then go suit up, my man. If all us men here gotta be miserable—" He shot a faux-panicked glance toward his wife. "I mean *happily* married..."

"Yeah, you better mean happily married," Remmy fired back at him playfully.

Nico sauntered over to her and slid his arms around her, trying to pick at the pastries. She batted his hand away. "No touching."

I left them then, took a shower, shaved, and dressed in the suit I'd picked out. I kept waiting for the nerves to kick in, but they never did.

When we were all suited and frocked up, we made the convoy down Stanning Road to my house. I still wasn't nervous. I just wanted it to be done. I wanted to be married already. I wanted to start my official forever with Lawson as soon as possible.

The plan was that we'd arrive at the house at four, and I'd walk in last, walk straight up the aisle to a waiting Lawson. So I waited inside the house and gave everyone plenty of time to take their seats. When I couldn't stand it any longer, I looked at Rosemary and gave her the nod. "It's time, girl."

I walked out the back with her and went to the side where the butterfly house stood. It had taken a good six months to plan, six months to build, and twelve months to establish what it was today.

I paused at the threshold for a deep breath, then opened the door, and Rosemary and I stepped inside.

There inside the butterfly house was Mum, Dad, April and Poppy, Remmy, Nico and Luka. On Lawson's side were his parents, Paterson and Bree, Mackellar and James, and they all turned to look at me.

The only person missing was Professor Warner Tillman. The old man had passed away a year ago. Lawson had been devastated and had not only lost his mentor but a dear friend. Lawson swore his legacy would live on, and I'd never been more grateful that Lawson had named the butterfly after him. The Tillman Copper would indeed live on.

But I couldn't take my eyes off the man at the front. Lawson. Looking incredible in his charcoal suit and bow tie, of course. He grinned when he saw me, and then I noticed the butterflies.

Dozens of Tillman Coppers fluttered above our heads. Lawson's butterfly house was now the largest living display of the Tillman Coppers in the world. When Warner Tillman had passed away, they'd moved the study to Lawson's facility. He bred many, and they flourished enough that he could release them.

We'd been on a few expeditions to find, research, save some butterflies all over the country, but these little copper-coloured butterflies would be not only Warner's legacy, but Lawson's too.

And the fact they were an integral part of our wedding was perfect. The celebrant standing near Lawson put her hand out and a butterfly landed on her, making her laugh. Luka had one land in his curly hair, and Hyacinth was trying to entice one onto her palm. Lawson had one on his shoulder, but he didn't seem to notice. He just stared at me.

I started to walk to him then, with Rosemary at my side. When I reached him, he held out his hand and I took it, sliding his palm into mine, in a feeling that was entirely of coming home. Rosemary sat at our feet, looking up at us both like she knew good and well what was going on.

The celebrant started her spiel then, only stopping every so often to appreciate a butterfly as it skipped across the air in front of her. Paterson's laughter interrupted her once, but he'd had a butterfly trying to land on his eyelid. It was an incredibly personal, private ceremony, with our closest family and friends. And butterflies, of course.

With our hands clasped, we exchanged plain silver wedding bands, and I promised to love and honour, cherish and adore him all my days.

Lawson's smile made my heart beat double time. "You'd once said you'd watched me become imago, getting my wings and being who I was born to be. But I could say the same about you. You keep telling me I've made you happier than any other time in your life, and I am grateful and humbled... and I, too, am witness to you becoming the man you were meant to be." He took a breath and squeezed my hands. "In entomology, we have a term we call *imagines*. It's the plural of imago. And if imago is one butterfly reaching its full potential, then surely we, together, would be *imagines*. I will love and honour you, cherish and adore you for all my days, Jack. Nothing would bring me greater joy than to be your husband."

I had to blink back tears, though I'm sure no one was fooled. I nodded. "And I yours."

The celebrant lifted her arm to show a butterfly on her sleeve, and with a smile, she declared us husband and husband.

Something shifted inside me, settled into place, and we kissed, sealing our ceremony done. We were quickly surrounded by our families with warm hugs and laughter while butterflies danced around our heads.

"I better go check on dinner," Remmy said, disappearing out the doors. We all followed her, leaving the butterflies to settle for the afternoon. We sat at our dining table and ate various pastries from baskets like we'd done on our very first date. We drank locally mulled cider too, then Nico's Portuguese tarts, laughing and celebrating.

We were heading to New Zealand for our honeymoon in a few days, and talk soon turned to that. "But there are earthquakes in New Zealand," Lawson's mum said.

"Or avalanches!" my mum added.

"It's not snowing," Lawson informed them. "And I'm not *that* accident prone. The bushfire wasn't exactly an accident, and the whole incident with the cane toad was simply a set of unfortunate circumstances..."

"And the time on Mount Kosciuszko?" Paterson furthered. "What was that?"

"It was slippery underfoot."

"And the time in the Blue Mountains?" Mackellar added with a smile.

Lawson lifted his chin. "Well, luckily for Jack—"

"Luckily for Jack?" his dad barked out a laugh. "Luckily for *you*!"

Lawson sighed and I leaned in and kissed him, trying not to smile. "I'll always be with you."

"Because the National Parks and Wildlife Service have banned him from visiting alone," Darren said.

It was all said in good fun, and the jibes at Lawson's run of bad luck whilst out in the field had long been a running family joke. But still, I put my arm around him and defended his honour. "I'll have you know, he's very capable and responsible."

Lawson gave me a look of love and thanks, then preened to his family. "Thank you, Jack."

But then I added, "Well, except for the bushfire thing."

"Uncle Lawson!" Luka came running in from out the back, Rosemary at his side. "Uncle Lawson, I think your butterflies have escaped."

"What?"

We shot up out of our seats and raced outside, but the butterfly house was fully sealed. There's no way any could have gotten out.

"No, over here," Luka cried. He was standing at the side of the house, waving us over. "Here they are."

It was the *Bursaria spinosa* shrub we'd planted after the bushfire. For three years it had thrived on the northern side of the house with the rosemary that Rosemary still loved. Lawson had kept an eye on it, the *Notoncus* ants had built a colony, but there had never been any butterflies...

Lawson crouched down in the dirt, still wearing his suit, and examined the foliage. He bent lower and inspected the roots of the shrub, then bent right down so his hands were in the dirt and he was looking at the undergrowth.

He pulled back, looked up at me, and grinned. That kind of heart-stopping grin that he only gave to me and butterflies.

"What?" I asked, though I was pretty sure I already knew.

He stood up slowly and looked at all of us waiting for him to speak. He barked out a happy laugh and put his hand over his mouth. "We have Tillman Coppers. In the wild. Here. *My* butterfly. In the wild at my house."

Everyone cheered, and I collected him in a crushing hug. "I knew you could do it."

He mumbled into my neck. "On our wedding day!"

"Like they somehow knew."

He nodded, and when he pulled back, he had tears in

his eyes. "Like Warner sent them here as a wedding gift. Do you think that's possible?"

I smiled and kissed him softly on the lips. "I think he's up there somewhere in the biggest butterfly house he could have dared imagined and sent them here to you, today of all days."

Lawson got all teary. "Thank you."

I noticed then that our families had left us alone to have this moment in private. Lawson put his fingers to my tie and adjusted the knot. He still had watery eyes, though it wasn't a sadness. More of an overwhelming love. "You look so handsome today," he whispered.

I ran my thumb over his jaw. "So do you."

"I wish Warner could have been here."

"He was," I said. Then I looked to the shrub and the roosting butterflies. "He is here."

"How do you always know exactly what to say?"

I shrugged. "I dunno, Lawson. You did pretty well with your vows today. I thought we agreed on no personal vows, then you surprised me with the whole speech on imagines?"

"Did you like that? I thought it was fitting for us."

"I loved it. And it was very fitting. If you were imago on your own, then we together are imagines."

He stared into my eyes and smiled. "Oh, Jack, that is where you're wrong. I was, could never be, imago on my own. If I ever did reach imago, it was only ever because of you."

I put my forehead to his and held his jaw. "Lawson Gale—"

"Lawson Brighton-Gale," he corrected with a smile.

I grinned at that. "Doctor Lawson Brighton-Gale."

"Yes, Jack Brighton-Gale?"

Dear God, I loved the sound of that. I put my fingers

under his chin and lifted his face. I put my eyelashes to his cheek and gave him butterfly kisses until he sighed. "We better get inside. Our families are waiting."

"Must we?" he asked dreamily. He glanced behind me to the setting sun, to the colours of the sky, then back to me. "I wouldn't mind starting our forever out here, just us. The sunset, the silence, just us."

"You forgot the butterflies."

He put his hand to his stomach and shook his head slowly. "Oh, no. I didn't."

Now I kissed his lips. "Imago?"

He shook his head again and smiled. "No. Imagines."

~ THE END

DELETED SCENE

JACK

~ When Jack goes with Lawson and Piers to drop off the samples at the CSIRO lab.

IT WASN'T that I didn't trust Piers... it was that... well, okay. I didn't trust him entirely. He had never exactly been encouraging of Lawson's theories and findings, to what end was anyone's guess. I just wanted to ensure the samples got to the CSIRO without incident. I wanted Lawson's work to be received, respected.

So the three of us had made the trip to the CSIRO building in Cairns. And as Lawson and Piers went through to the lab area, I took a seat in the waiting room. It was then a face on a years-old magazine on the side table caught my attention. I couldn't believe it...

God, I hadn't seen him in years.

But that face was unforgettable. Well, one face was. There were three men standing together at some rural meeting, but the one guy in the middle hadn't changed in years. Still ruggedly handsome, still had that killer smile.

I'd spent *personal time* with him during our uni days in Sydney. Meaning we'd spent a lot of time in bed together. He was a country kid, far from home, as was I. We had a few classes together, both of us environmental science students, two out of towners, both spreading our gay wings for the first time.

He'd disappeared during our third year, apparently had to go home, back to the farm, and never graduated. I hadn't seen him since. But he'd obviously done all right for himself. The magazine was a *Beef Farmers Association* edition titled *Farming in the Future.*

I hadn't thought of him in so long.

I flipped the magazine open and started reading about farming the remote Outback deserts in the twenty-first century. Wow, he'd really done well for himself.

In all our time together, he never spoke much about his life back home. Every time conversation turned to family, he'd clam up, and I could read cues well enough to know it was a subject best left alone. Not that we were that close. Truth be told, we didn't do a great deal of talking when we were together... I knew he was from some huge property in the middle of the desert, but I really had no idea just how big. Jesus Christ, his property was about the same size as all of Tasmania. Okay, so maybe not quite that big, but jeez... I had no idea.

The article went on to talk about using technology and how this new generation of farmers were doing this better, smarter than their fathers before them. It was an interesting read. It was such a blast from the past! I couldn't believe out of all the waiting rooms, out of all the magazines, I had to see this one. The magazine itself was a few years old, worn and tattered, and I wondered how he was doing now.

But it wasn't long before Lawson and Piers came back out. Lawson was smiling, that happy, heart-stopping smile and any past lovers were soon forgotten.

"You ready to go camping out?" Lawson asked excitedly.

I threw the magazine back on the pile, stood up, and matched his grin with my own. Spending the night in the middle of the forest with Lawson sounded bloody perfect to me. "Sure am."

~fin

SPECIAL MENTION TO JULIE BOZZA

I'd like to offer a heartfelt thanks to Julie Bozza. For offering her support, feedback, and input for the Imago series.

Readers, if you enjoyed Imago and Imagines, please do yourself a favour and pick up Julie's Butterfly Hunter. You won't be disappointed.
Nicholas and Dave are gorgeous.

ABOUT THE AUTHOR

N.R. Walker is an Australian author, who loves her genre of
gay romance.
She loves writing and spends far too much time doing it, but
wouldn't have it any other way.

She is many things: a mother, a wife, a sister, a writer. She
has pretty, pretty boys who live in her head, who don't let
her sleep at night unless she gives them life with words.

She likes it when they do dirty, dirty things... but likes it
even more when they fall in love.

She used to think having people in her head talking to her
was weird, until one day she happened across other writers
who told her it was normal.

She's been writing ever since...

Contact the Author
nrwalker@nrwalker.net

ALSO BY N.R. WALKER

BLIND FAITH

Blind Faith

Through These Eyes (Blind Faith #2)

Blindside: Mark's Story (Blind Faith #3)

Ten in the Bin

Point of No Return – Turning Point #1

Breaking Point – Turning Point #2

Starting Point – Turning Point #3

Element of Retrofit – Thomas Elkin Series #1

Clarity of Lines – Thomas Elkin Series #2

Sense of Place – Thomas Elkin Series #3

Taxes and TARDIS

Three's Company

Red Dirt Heart

Red Dirt Heart 2

Red Dirt Heart 3

Red Dirt Heart 4

Red Dirt Christmas

Cronin's Key

Cronin's Key II

Cronin's Key III

Exchange of Hearts

The Spencer Cohen Series, Book One

The Spencer Cohen Series, Book Two

The Spencer Cohen Series, Book Three

The Spencer Cohen Series, Yanni's Story

Blood & Milk

The Weight Of It All

A Very Henry Christmas (The Weight of It All 1.5)

Perfect Catch

Switched

Imago

Imagines

Red Dirt Heart Imago

On Davis Row

Finders Keepers

Evolved

Galaxies and Oceans

Titles in Audio:

Cronin's Key

Cronin's Key II

Cronin's Key III

Red Dirt Heart

Red Dirt Heart 2

Red Dirt Heart 3

Red Dirt Heart 4

The Weight Of It All

Switched

Point of No Return

Breaking Point

Starting Point

Spencer Cohen Book One

Spencer Cohen Book Two

Spencer Cohen Book Three

Yanni's Story

On Davis Row

Free Reads:

Sixty Five Hours

Learning to Feel

His Grandfather's Watch (And The Story of Billy and Hale)

The Twelfth of Never (Blind Faith 3.5)

Twelve Days of Christmas (Sixty Five Hours Christmas)

Best of Both Worlds

Translated Titles:

Fiducia Cieca (Italian translation of Blind Faith)

Attraverso Questi Occhi (Italian translation of Through These Eyes)

Preso alla Sprovvista (Italian translation of Blindside)

Il giorno del Mai (Italian translation of Blind Faith 3.5)

Cuore di Terra Rossa (Italian translation of Red Dirt Heart)

Cuore di Terra Rossa 2 (Italian translation of Red Dirt Heart 2)

Cuore di Terra Rossa 3 (Italian translation of Red Dirt Heart 3)

Cuore di Terra Rossa 4 (Italian translation of Red Dirt Heart 4)

Intervento di Retrofit (Italian translation of Elements of Retrofit)

Confiance Aveugle (French translation of Blind Faith)

A travers ces yeux: Confiance Aveugle 2 (French translation of Through These Eyes)

Aveugle: Confiance Aveugle 3 (French translation of Blindside)

À Jamais (French translation of Blind Faith 3.5)

Cronin's Key (French translation)

Cronin's Key II (French translation)

Au Coeur de Sutton Station (French translation of Red Dirt Heart)

Partir ou rester (French translation of Red Dirt Heart 2)

Faire Face (French translation of Red Dirt Heart 3)

Trouver sa Place (French translation of Red Dirt Heart 4)

Rote Erde (German translation of Red Dirt Heart)

Rote Erde 2 (German translation of Red Dirt Heart 2)

www.ingramcontent.com/pod-product-compliance
Lightning Source LLC
Chambersburg PA
CBHW050531190726
48284CB00003B/1032